Echo 4

Donut Hole the Battle

The Marine Battle of Echo 4 During the TET Offensive 1968

R.C. Le Beau

The small Compound of Echo 4 is surrounded by three battalions of VC and NVA that are tasked to take down the Da Nang airbase hence the Donut and the Hole

This story is about that battle; not only is Echo 4 surrounded, but so is their enemy.

The Novel is Based on the Biography of the book "Donut Hole"

R.C. Le Beau

ISBN: 978-1-915165-35-0

RC LE BEAU

Dedication

The dedication is to those who lost their lives during this war and battle. But also to the Armed Forces of the Vietnam war. The Vietnamese suffered the most from over a thousand years of war in their country. Also, the families who suffered from losing their loved ones fought and died on this land. No matter who wins the battle, the land still belongs to the Vietnamese people in the end. The conclusion of the Vietnam War would be this one. With all due respect to its people. But ultimately, the Vietnamese people won the war. Your sacrifices did pay off in the end, with your peace and no more occupations from other counties on your land to fight for your resources, which rightfully belonged to you. God bless.

Acknowledgment

The battle of Echo 4 is in his Biography of the book Donut Hole with all its references and AAR (After Action Reports); the battle action itself, which was historical, was hard to explain in a Biography. With that in mind, the best way to bring forward that battle is with this novel, "Donut Hole the Battle." It will allow me to write a different context and narrative for the reader. To get the feel of that battle of Echo 4. I would also like to mention that this novel is upfront and personal, with action as close as words will allow me to be.

To tell this story, I respectfully tell a Marine war story. But also acknowledge, this is a story of both Marines and the Army fighting together with an unknown enemy size in the Da Nang area with what was to be a simple task of releasing the pressure of the small compound of Echo 4's peril. The TET Offensive had tasked MACV and III MAF to defend the Da Nang airbase. The Marines at Echo 4 were fighting an enemy of unknown size in the early morning hours of February 8th. At that time, everyone was caught flat-footed, with a high volume of resistance from the enemy surrounding Echo 4. That resistance stopped the relieving force of the 3rd Battalion 5th Marines and the Army's Americal Division's newly formed Task Force Miracle,

Companies A, B, C, and D, landing by air from Chu Lai to the south of the Da Nang airbase along Highway 1.

Much research went into this book for the accuracy of this war story. Also, this war story is of first and third-person telling, with accurate embellishments as needed to tell the story. To be precise, the feeling of combat in the Vietnam war. It uses the language and the character's attitude before, during, and after the battle. The horrors of warfare are the creations of PTSD, which wartime veterans suffer every day of their lives. The narrative in this book will spark the reader's feelings with all the contradictions of war. Like 100 people go to battle, 100 different tales of that same battle come forward. And all this is acknowledged, but the risk is worth telling the tale of. Like Marine Col. Oliver North once famously said, "This is a battle and war story that needs to be told."

RC LeBeau, author of the book "Donut Hole," is now the author of "Echo 4 the battle," the Novel.

About the Author

He lives in northern California near the San Francisco Bay area. His first book was a Biography bearing the name, Donut Hole with the subject of his life and the Vietnam war. The lone survivor of his immediate family of his late older brother Joe and his mother and father. His stroke at this time in his life came with time to spare and write books.

This is the first novel he wrote focused on his Marine Corps war experiences that changed his life forever. Although his being an Author is a newfound shingle on his door, it also brings relief to telling his stories late in life. His work has paid off with 4–5-star ratings on Amazon. His readers wanted more. Biographies are personable, but his storytelling has just begun and has been well received.

Since he has had a fascinating life that he has lived, he says this may be just the beginning of stories to be told. Since his first book appeared two years ago, he has also been encouraged to write more by some well-known authors, screenplay writers, and producers. They said they would like to see more, maybe a novel, which he has done here with this book.

R.C. Le Beau

[Blank Page Intentionally]

CONTENTS

Preface

Vietnam 1968, the Vietnamese holiday TET started on January 31st, 1968, which is no different from previous TET holidays. It is their Chinese New Year, which is every year. The U.S. occupation has increased substantially across the country. And with that said, action in the field has increased also. During this holiday, Command has determined a stand down of war activity in the country was in line with previous years. That will allow for some peace for everyone. MAC V had some intel that there might be some action this holiday and since our enemy, who doesn't use Command and control too much over their Radio systems, will use physical communications instead. We were under strict orders not to fire unless you were fired on. This disengage order was countrywide. Our home FLC base outside and north of Da Nang by 5 miles was no different. However, we're instructed to play a Hollywood special effects game of our base being attacked the day before the TET holiday. That was to be played out with several bases across the country to simulate attacks on our bases at a specific time after dusk. So, G-2 put empty barrels around with kerosene and little gas, with a small charge to explode at different locations. Of course, this didn't work for the most part, and it was a peaceful night for everyone. The next day and night were quite different. But we Marines at FLC really didn't know much about how the enemies were doing across the country. The early parts of battles on Jan 30th were happening all around our base. We had also learned that parts of Da Nang had been overrun, and the Marines instructed and restricted from leaving our base.

Marine CAP units were small compounds dotted around the I Corps area. Their jobs were to provide security for different villages, medical care, and training for local PFs (Popular Forces) to help fend off the local VC if attacked. The Seabees had built some great bunkers to withstand mortar attacks and small armed weapons in the mix. Then these compounds were surrounded by 40 to 60 feet of wire entanglements, with booby traps mixed in, flare trip wires, and a cleared field of fire around that. Rice paddies were suitable for that open ground. Defendable? Yes. But, to hold off an effort attack? No. Just enough to hold off, invasion, and then call-in artillery and air support. At least, that was the plan.

At Echo 4 was surrounded, and if you took a minigun and blasted it at our compound. The results would have been the same. The bagged bunkers had interlocking patterns, and the material did not rip so quickly, so bullets and shrapnel would not turn these bunkers into a pile of sand. However, at Echo 4, we had so many hits from bullets and shrapnel. The drooping of sandbags told the tail of our battle at Echo4. The struggle was outrageous and intense.

This story of 11 or so Marines and half dozen PFs will talk about that battle, our little hornets' nest. But remember this, when you are in the trees, you don't see the forest. The distraction from 3/5 Marines and the Army's Task Force was enough to pull our enemy off us. So, in other words, sitting at home, you don't know what is happening in the next neighborhood. It lasted a day and a half, and for that time frame, the Army not far from us had casualties for one day, only second to the later infamous battle of Hamburger Hill. This story is about all units involved in this battle, I called "Donut Hole", the Battle." By RC LeBeau.

Echo 4

Page Blank Intentionally

Chapter 1

Vietnam Just Before The 68 Tet Offensive

I visited my older self just as you are visiting me. It had been so long that I had forgotten the exact day, but I had not forgotten the details. They were still very much a part of me. All I needed was a reminder, a trigger, and that reminder came very quickly when I stopped and thought about it.

Darkness—dense, thick, growing in front of me. Deep-space dark. The darkness gnaws at me, wide-eyed, as though it was surprising to find me looking at this place in my mind. I would zoom in, and far away, a prick of light catches my eye. My head swivels, back to front, like an owl, as I look closely at this stroke of light that had caught my eye in this darkness, like a mussel flash. A foggy night with a distant streetlight hanging in the fog, glowing like a flare hanging there but not swaying back and forth, which normally happens with flares in the sky.

I feel a familiar rattle and jolt as I look at in the sky. There was a stream of big birds in the trees, flapping their wings and cracklings in the air as they took flight from the sudden crack of lightning and thunder, rushing away in groups.

Their flight was a warning of what was maybe the enemy about to come our way, but no, it wasn't, just birds.

This January… and a storm front? Not, it was just an outgoing 105 gun, firing from a nearby battery, rushing rounds off to a place of death and destruction, with a faint boom somewhere else.

The clouds are getting heavier by the second, and the sky is getting darker. And soon enough, I started to hear the rhythmic sounds of soft tapping on the porch-roof above me. Raindrops began to tap the crumples on the floorboard as the twigs and branches rustled overhead. The leaves were now blowing in full swing, and even though I was sitting under a shade, some leaves had made their way onto me. I wipe the wet leaves from my trousers and jacket, the shirt splattered with rain drops. The rain had caught more momentum. The once slowly dipping drops were now bouncing off the ground, almost reaching my face, the air now smothered by the stink of rotten leaves and muddy puddles that were forming in front of me.

Every time I heard drops on the steps, my heart rate went up,

One after the other, the rain brings memories of the past that envelops me inside. These memories felt like a lifetime ago, a life I remembered nothing of. I try to flee the situation and go inside. I got to my feet awkwardly, but as I stood on the floorboard that was wet with rainwater, I started swaying a little. Before I could regain my balance, there was a crack of thunder and a flash of light.

The thunder rings, distant, insistent.

Feeling the first touch of panic, I jolt upright. My throat tightens, breaths coming loud and fast.

I don't move. I don't breathe.

Be calm. I told myself, but I could not. The memories were knocking, and I had to answer sooner or later or sooner —perhaps—no, not perhaps—quite certainly: I had to answer my knocking memories.

Because rain, for me, isn't simply raining. The thunder that comes along with this brutal rain is also a cold reminder: it reminds me of yesterdays that were many moons ago, one year before many years. I don't want to think of it. Not now and not later. But as I sit on my chair, I can't think of anything else. Anxiety tweaks the vague nerve as I hear the second rumble of thunder. A sickish shrinking from the past comes knocking me, like the wind that was running past me at full speed from somewhere out there, that is followed by a flash of light...

A light that reminds me of a day I don't want to go back to, home, sweet home in Michigan. Then I wake up with my fan blowing on me. Wow, it was only a dream of my future self.

It feels strange to say it out loud, it feels strange to acknowledge it as though I'm calling fate down upon myself, but if I'm to survive Vietnam, I'll need to live every day without fear. That was the lesson I taught myself the first day. Sleep is my time machine, my transporter to a life I once had or will have. But now I am back to the here and now, Vietnam. Day of January 28th, 1968

Marine Corps base FLC is about five miles north of Da Nang along Hwy 1 near the white sanded beach of Da Nang Bay, with Monkey Mountain off to the right and Hai Gia Mountain to the left. Across highway 1 is the small Seabees base, which had beachfront property. Further north down highway 1 was the fishing village called Namo and a bridge north of that where Hwy 1 shared the bridges, one lane of traffic moving north or south. On the north side of that bridge was a Marine compound guarding the bridge and river entrances to and from the bay into the land.

Back at the FLC base, things are busy, as expected. Local traffic is getting active, and trucks are leaving and entering the three main gates. Weather, the morning fog had just burned off and turned into partly cloudy skies. Inland Vietnam was hot, muggy, and hard to breathe; either way, sweat was always your friend, just like rain and heat. If it were not your friend, it would piss you off all the time. Shaking my head, I take a step away from all that heat and humidity.

I was suffering from a heat rash under my arms between my legs and I had found Listerine, which burned like hell, but it worked better than the ointments they gave me at our base Med center or sick bay. "It burns," I whispered to myself quietly as I tended to my water blister.

The rash didn't look painful, but jolting pain throbbed up my arm as sweat stood out on my forehead.

"Hey RC, how are you doing?" a passing Marine said.

I was not in the mood to answer even a harmless greet, so with irritation running in all my veins, I grunted at him with a not-so-pleasant remark. "It's not for you to worry," I retorted.

"Are you sure?" He asked a rather rhetorical question. "Because I see you're in a lot of pain,"

I watch him. I glare.

He glares back.

"I'm not," I dismissed the claims, but a passerby was not letting me have my moment.

"You know, it's a common belief that Marines can override any pain in the body." He teased me as I felt myself aching with anger.

I drew a breath, then another, trying to suppress my anger, but the burning of my rash was burning my heart…and my speech.

"Fuck you, Ramirez," I almost barked as he laughed because he knew my heat rash had made me walk funny, but it was healing, thank God. If it wasn't healing, I would have been the most annoying person here by a mile.

"Okay, okay, I'll get out of your hair," Ramirez says as he looks at me with a smirk.

"Please." I gaze deep into his eyes. "Thank you."

He sighs and walks away.

If I weren't already, I would have gotten cranky, irritated, angry, and just bitter.

It's Sunday, January 28th, 1968, I am walking down the base main drag to the motor pool to pick up my PC (Personal Carrier), like a non-armored pickup truck that seats 4 in the rear truck bed, and one can sit up front, just enough for a Marine fire team. When I get there, I see my PC washed and oil changed, as this Marine goes down the list. I walked around and said, "hey, Marine, where are my two new tires?" He answers, "They're not in yet." I ask, "What about all those new trucks parked on the road?" He replies, "They just arrived over the weekend on Saturday."

A Marine in need is a Marine in deed, I thought to myself, this is a logistical grey area in a war zone.

So, I drive over to the new trucks, and at this moment, I take the new wheels off the new truck's door-mounted spare tires and put them in the back of my truck bed. Problem solved. Ideally, all military truck wheels are the same size. I go to the base supply office to meet with my commander Captain James for orders.

Master Sargent Borders is to my left, and across a walkway to my right is Captain James. I salute and say,

"L/Cpl. LeBeau is reporting for duty, sir." Capt. James returns the salute and says, "At ease LeBeau." I reply, "Yes, sir." M.Sgt. Borders behind me says, "Have you taken care of that rash, LeBeau?" I nod my head fervently and reply, "It's getting better Top.",

"Good. That's good,",

There's a pause for a while, and then after thinking for a little while, he says. "I know you're recovering, but you are still going to An-Hoa, and our new Lt. Willis will accompany you,"

"Oh," I say as I think back to the last time I had made that trip. Fair to say it wasn't much of a success. But before I could contest his decision, captain James put my mind to ease.

"But you need not worry. This time you're not going to go by truck, this time, you'll use a chopper. We don't want you to risk being caught in a mob of traffic. There's already too much enemy activity between here and there right now. LeBeau",

"Yes, sir." I nod my head without any objections,

"Choppers are hard to come by right now, so I will let you know as soon as possible."

That's when SGT interferes, "LeBeau, I want you to go over to the warehouse across the street and help them with the Forklift moving things around. Then tonight, you with

7

Clutch Platoon will have guard duty on the perimeter all night; see Sgt. Ski for details."

"Alright, Top." I nodded, thinking I understood.

"Now get out of here." LeBeau, "Yes, top."

All is silent for a while.

Then I leave the room.

But as I walk out, I stop and look at Borders, "Hey, Top...."

"What?" When he looked back at me, his voice had softened. But his features were still hard.

"Listerine works well on heat rash. It burns like hell, but it works." Borders smile to himself with a look of self-satisfaction.

"Ok, Thanks, I'll try that; now get out of here."

It started raining, and all of us in Vietnam knew to keep everything wrapped in cellophane. The strong caress of the wind was enough to blow everything away, so it was more of a curse than a blessing.

The truck went by, splashing a mud puddle on me, but it didn't matter; I was already wet head to toe. The rain was steady but not hard, so running made no sense. The rain on the metal roof was almost deafening anyway in the warehouse. The sergeant in the warehouse said, "Good LeBeau, go get the Forklift outside. Leave your Rifle, Helmet, Flak Jacket, and suspender utility belt here at my desk." LeBeau, "Yes, Sgt."

Later, toward the end of the day, Clutch Platoon gathered at the guard shack and waited for Platoon Gunny Sgt. Campbell for our brief.

I had just seized a fistful of Listerine and towels when the SGT called.

What were the odds of that happening?

Intel at S-2 Command, we knew something was up, with him being late at the round-up. Then these Marines showed up in a truck and loaded us up with frags, ammo, pop-flares, smoke, and PRC'25 radios, and something was definitely up. We checked each other for proper placement. Com Marines were checking the radios, some screeching, then silence. This is starting to get highly unusual. Still, a light rain was coming down and pattering on everything. Then came Gunny, briskly in the storm and dark, with street and base lights in the background. Everyone scrambled to assemble a Platoon formation.

As I examined him, he examined the room and those who were inside: Gunny yelled; gather around me, squad leaders, fire team leaders close to me.

Nobody pays attention except me. And, a low growl, like a quiet motor, escaped his lips.

"Listen up!" he yells. This time with anger.

But the platoon was not ready.

Staff Sgt. Wolf, annoyed without reaction, yelled louder than him, "In other words, stop whatever the fuck you're doing and shut the fuckup."

And in an instant, for a moment, everyone is silent. Gunny looked at the SGT and nodded at him as a gesture of thank-you as he began to speak.

"You are now reinforced and equipped, and this is why. Charlie might have plans for us tonight. Magazines in the well, but do not, I repeat, do not chamber a round in the breach—lock and load, when necessary, only, or on command. No one will fire your weapon unless fired upon. Is that clear? The lieutenant will check every Marine for safety and orders to each post. Radio orders will be given to the leaders, and they will give you orders. Is that clear? Platoon,"

"Yes, Gunny." He wrinkles his nose.

"Capt. James is in command and will direct the Platoon accordingly. Is that clear?"

"Yes, Gunny," Platoon answered, and Gunny smiled.

His voice perked the way it does when he's thinking out loud.

"Good. Now here is what is going on. TET is a Vietnamese holiday, but this holiday may be different. So, we are doubling the guard. We have set up some mortars around the base and Miked in the locations outside the wire. Three 4 hours watch, leaders figure that accordingly."

"My only advice is…be careful?" He smiles a bit, a cautious smile with one corner of his mouth tipping upward and another forming a frown.

"Yes, sir," I answered with complete conviction, but I knew there was more than just care and luck that we needed. It was madness to be in this city without that caution in our minds. And that caution had started ringing again tonight.

The war currently has Khe Shan surrounded by two divisions of NVA, which have received at least 1500 incoming daily rounds since January 21st. The Army has been moving north along highway 1 for a week, with companies staying here at FLC. It will also bolster our defense if need be. However, hopefully, this TET holiday will not need that type of defense. Hopefully, everything will be okay, and this day will pass without no incidents or casualties.

I'm thinking we are fully capable of defending this Base and the surrounding area ourselves, but their presence is welcome. They are camped out all over our Base and enjoying our Mess Hall's food. Much better than C-Rations; it is popularly known that C-Rats taste like shit. It included the issue of two 6-ounce (170 g) cans of fruit for two meals to replace the one 12-ounce (340 g) can be issued for one meal in the C-3 ration. The C-Ration box numbers indicated which C-Rations were more likable than others. Also, smokers chose filters instead of non-filtered cigarettes because the tobacco was so dry from aging that it sometimes fell apart, besides the filters were great ear blockers.

Troops would be supplied six cans per day, with two cans for each meal. This is what we were supposed to eat, and as I went through the ration, my stomach started to rumble, and I realized that I hadn't eaten anything all day.

My best bet was the food of the C-Ration was B3A1's

They were supposed to update the C-Rations with three, excuse the term, "Main dishes." And one which they detested the most was Corned Beef Hash, which Marines called dog food. But hungry dogs won't eat it. This lack of variety produced what was termed "C ration fatigue." by commanders, we Marines called it "just plain food poisoning, with nasty smokes." So, our Army visitors were in seventh heaven with our food.

Canned fruit, canned fruit cocktails, canned baked goods like pound cake and cinnamon nut rolls, and canned meat items like ham slices and turkey loaf were our favorites, but we'd rarely get them. For us, heaven was just getting food; good food was a myth and blessing we mortals only dreamt about, but K-Rations were better.

Bunkers and our Base

Our bunker system is fanned, spread out, and well laid around our base perimeter with interlocking fields of fire, with high and low bunker types. The Seabees have made some well-engineered bunkers with com wire communications and battery-operated radios. In addition to exposed fighting holes, sandbagged placements intertwined between the more giant bunkers. Outside our wire is a chain link fence jointed to our white-sanded base bunkered entrances.

I might add those starlight systems are in the bunker mix, giving us access to the new green-light night vision. Seismic detection devices are wired into our bunkers to detect crawling and walking sapper-type enemies and animals. The Seabees bunkers also included a protruding wood awning of our cinemascope openings for an authentic view of our battlefront. It also helped to kept the weather out. Several hundred sandbags were interlocking, with a rip-stop designed cloth that could take direct hits without falling apart much.

It is a considerable base layout. The perimeter had a great field of fire to the north. The west defense chain-link fence was way beyond the kill zone of the bunkers, along the road of Highway one, and looking at the beautiful Da Nang Bay. That linked up to the low trip wire of our northern defense system. The western chain-link fence skirting the highway linked up to the southern fence line, which was unique because there was no wire entanglement, and the southern perimeter fence line had a large Vietnamese refugee camp up to the fence. Their backyards came up against our chain-link fence south of the line. It linked up to our eastern chain-link fence line. Our eastern side of our Base was unique also because there was no wire entanglement, and there was a road entrance and gate that led to a roadside village called Boom, Boom Ville. This road made a connection to the Marine 11th Engineer's Base. It also went south, a backroad through the refugee camp, connecting to highway one, the southeast, and then to the south to Da Nang. Why does all this matter? Well, no reason, but you get the picture of FLC's Base.

Arriving at my assigned bunker at the south end of the Base, we were deciding who would have the first watch. I wasn't tired, so I volunteered for the last watch from 4 to 8 am, considered a critical watch that no buddy wanted it.

I want RC to have the last watch, Cpl. Ramirez said, "Bingo, I got it." The benefit of the last watch was that you got four hours-time off the next morning and could go to work after lunch. Nothing happened, and the com-line or radio on my watch. It was like a private radio program among Marines, sometimes fascinating, but mostly not.

We visit places of home in our imaginations once a week to help us live life or, as I like to say, hate our lives because many Marines like to brag and provide updates on their sexual adventures, which are about as exciting as watching paint dry or listening to grass growing.

One Marine online with a southern ascent feeling lonely for his wife said, "I would lay 12,000 miles of com-wire just to hear her my wife fart." And every Marine on the Com laughed.

I turn around, my eyes cast down, and I look away as my ears have heard that before.

I replied, "If it was my last day on earth, I would not want it to be here with you, Marines. I would want my last day on this earth to be with my woman fucking her with a heart attack of pleasure. That's the last thing I would like to do." Everyone laughed on the wire.

Chapter 2
Day before TET
Noon January 29th, 1968.

My day started with Armed Forces Radio blaring in the background at 11:00 in the morning. Hanoi Hanna had better music though.

The deafening back-ground noise of the radio that was far from ideal. It was not how I or anyone wanted to start their mornings. I had to wrench myself away from being away from and that of other-worldly chores of eating and sleeping in order to be here in the Nam with the work that has to be done.

As I got on with my morning, I went on my way to get my hair cut, passing all the mama sons who were smiling with their black teeth exposed. Knowing Command would never hire young Vietnamese girls without black teeth. If something like would happen, the outcome of "scandals" would be inevitable. Because every young Marine on Base would want to be fu*king them. One of the things we left behind was our loved ones. And that meant our wives and girlfriends, and this is what our young blood was craving. We all wanted someone, just for the sake of it, and this

Vietnamese hooch black-toothed cleaning ladies were not one of them. But taking them to your bed just wasn't possible. Even though ladies ruled our wildest fantasies and imagination, they were the forbidden fruit we weren't allowed to consume. These ladies didn't speak much English, and fucking them would get you a Court Marshall in a heartbeat, and if they yelled rape, you would pay a big fine, brig, criminalized, and sent home in disgrace, while the girls would get a cash bonus.

So put...putting my hands on them was definitely not in the cards.

You had to control the "brain" that was in your pants. And keep your hands off, no matter how horny you are. Besides all that, they weren't exactly angels. To be honest, they were ugly black-toothed chicks, and they were things that nightmares are made of, the black teeth worked for the most part.

So, as I juggled with these thoughts, I opened the screen door, "Hey, SSgt. Benson, what happening? What happened to all our Barbers?"

With a solemn face, Benson responded with a reply I was surprised to hear. "They got killed in a firefight last week. These dumb asses tried to ambush some Marines outside of Nam O. You were there Marine. You didn't know?" RC, "Fuck no, at night, you can't see shit, and in the heat of battle, I'm not checking out the dead gooks, just to see who we just killed in their hide. We had those two new Marines WIA, but thank God; no KIA's after an hour of holy-shit moments." Benson, "Ya, well, two of our favorite Barbers are gone. These two here are the smart ones." The Barbers smiled. LeBeau, "Nothing was going on last night on guard duty either. After this haircut, I'm going to shower and chow down." Benson, "Well, have a good one, RC. See Ya around. Don't forget rifle inspection at 17,00 hrs. next to the Quasit Huts."

Gunny Campbell stopped me at the Mess Hall and told me to get my PC truck, head over to the off-base Lumberyard, and pick up the latest signed inventory sheets for him and Captain James. After picking up my vehicle, I decided to take the back road through the 11th Marine Engineers base instead of the busy Hwy 1 and avoid all the traffic of military and human traffic. Of course, when I get there, the papers are not ready yet since the Lumberyard is located just along a downward northern finger of Freedom hill. The significant Da Nang PX location is next to Freedom hill. A series of smaller hills formed a saddle, with a dirt road passing to Mortar valley on the other side. I asked the Sgt. if he needed anything from the PX. And he replied, "No."

This allowed me to see my Vietnamese honey on the way back. It turned out to be a nice day, the PX was very busy, and I ran into SGT. Dennis Hammond. Dennis wanted to buy a Corvette when he got home and loved fishing. He was from a local CAP compound south of the Airbase along Hwy. 1 heading south. We were both getting short; this was his second tour in the Nam. We talked for a while, and he told me what a kickback compound he was on, and being stuck with this CAP unit pissed him off because he wanted action. That was his motivation for his second tour, along with his love of the Vietnamese people. I told him I would stop by his CAP unit when I traveled to the combat bases south of Da Nang and Happy valley with my PC. Little did I know, that would be the last time I would see Dennis alive. He said the village next to his compound would not be celebrating TET.

On my way back to the Lumberyard, I decided to stop by and see my Vietnamese girlfriend. I had not seen her for a few months. Fortunately for me, she wasn't like the other girls. She was beautiful, with long black hair, no black teeth, and a fantastic body, with a great sense of humor. Always wearing traditional Vietnamese clothing, I might add that she was also very clean. She never told me her age, but I believe she was in her early twenties, even though she looked much younger. She worked at a local Bazaar, where a group of Vietnamese people would sell food, soft drinks, and services, like a blind man playing his traditional Vietnamese four string instrument with Gored on the end, for Vietnamese money. There was also a Vietnamese dwarf who shined your boots; I chuckled. He did do a dam good job. She had a place where you could set down on lawn chairs, eat, drink and talk. She could speak Vietnamese, French, and a little English. She could speak my language, just not too well but cute.

The best part was her personality, which was warm, brilliant, and aimed to, please. The weekends were the busiest, and military personnel from all over the Da Nang came.

She said, "Many military men would offer her money for sex. Some men would even ask for her hand in marriage. Then she quietly said, "I never would ever accept them because her man, he would have to be an extra special man for her." After a few months of talking with me, she said, "I was that special one for her." With that, about a month ago, she gave me a handwritten map to visit her place and meet her family.

She had a well-built home, very clean, on a big open lot. My Marine friends did not know of her as I did. Almost everyone talked about her and said she was a VC spy. Under these wartime experiences, she may be, but she loved me and never asked me anything about the war. Her father fought and died with the French Foreign Legionnaires in the early fifties. They had lived in Da Nang ever since she could remember.

I pulled into her circle driveway, waited, and she came running out, smiling and happy. "Hi, RC." As she jumped into the front seat excitedly.

I say, with comparatively less excitement than her.

"Hi, sweetheart." She kisses me and says, "What a pleasant surprise, my love." I say, "Are you sure?" She smiles and says, "No, I'm not sure. I will leave now." then she laughs and says, "It has been a long time since I see you. I was afraid something happened to you, my love." I wonder if she really loved me for real or because was it that I had a French name, but I do feel her love maybe genuine. She says something in French, then in English, "You look like you have lost more weight. I said, "No, I've been eating ok, but very busy and burning off what I eat, sweetheart. She points to the top of Freedom hill and says, "I want to go to our favorite spot up there with you. Please, can we go?" I looked at her and said, "Ok, but not long because I'm still working, sweetheart." She smiles and says, "Ok, let's hurry and go."

It takes a while to go up this cleared Tank Road leading up this big hill. In a four-wheel drive, I could easily make it to the top of this narrow north finger of Freedom hill. At the top, one can see over the Lumberyard and the nearby pass, with the Da Nang area spread out around the bay, with the FLC base off in the distant bay coastline north. But the view is unobstructed in all directions. It is room temperature, with a 5,000 ft. ceiling of clouds, as we spread out my poncho, with my camo blanket liner on top. The ground pitched downward slightly, making it a perfect lounging area away from the PC, with a light warm breeze. This vantage point also gives a great view of the Airbase, with a cloud-shrouded Monkey Mtn. in the distance and Marble Mtn. to its right. Happy valley goes further to the right and south and westward, then further to the right again, sandwiched between two Mtn. Ranges is Mortar valley running northward. What a great safe view of the war, with smoke streaming up from different locations in this panoramic view of the southwest and the distant sounds of war. The only word I can think of right now is mesmerizing, beautiful, and dangerous. You can't help but stare at its beauty, and what a wonderful place it would be to visit one day when the war is over, I said to myself.

By this point, I saw tears in my girlfriend's eyes. Out of concern, I tend to her, "What's wrong, sweetheart? What are all those tears about?" I asked. She replies, "I am afraid of losing you, the best man in my life." She said that, followed by something in French and Vietnamese. Then she says, "It's not fair; it's just not fair. I just feel like I'm going to lose you to this war. No matter what happens to you or me, you will never forget me." Sadly, "Will you? I'm the one who loves you." I think she must have been somewhat confused as to what to say…who I was and how she should behave with me.

She was attached to me, and I could see it in her eyes.

She looks at me briefly and says, "I want to have your baby. Marriage doesn't matter. If you give me your baby, I will have you inside of me if I lose you. Do you understand?" At that moment, we make mad passionate love with each other. Time has stopped. After a while, I noticed blood on her and me. I asked her, "Are you alright, sweetheart?" She replied, "Yes, my love, I am a virgin, and it hurts so good, sweetheart. Thank you for giving me the wish I have been waiting for all my life." Suddenly, big rounds are streaking high over our heads, with a distant rumbling gun noise. I told her that it was a 50-Cal. Zeroing in on our location. She panicky says to me, "How can they see us?" I reply, "They can't, but they can see the truck." I told her, "Go down the Tank trail. I'll get the Truck."

More rounds trailed high in the air, but lower than before; shit, what a fucking time to be targeted by a 50 Cal. machine gun. I'm moving fast and low to the truck.

I open the truck driver's door, and a round goes through the front windshield, punches through with a clack, and slaps through the olive-green canvasback in a split second on the Trucks driver's side. I yell, "Fuck." With my left hand, I pushed down on the clutch pedal forward and grabbed the shift stick to put it in neutral with my right hand. Now I can make the Truck move backward, then hand on the seat backward, thus moving the Truck back to point downhill on the road. I turned the steering wheel to turn the Truck around. I yell, "Fuck, this thing is heavy." More rounds are coming in and hitting on the dirt in the same spot where I was, and now I have to move forward to go down the hill. More bullets are hitting the ground. Shit, the fucker is following me. With the Truck rolling along now, I hop in the front seat, and speed is getting faster and faster. With the motor not running, this is not easy. I pass my lady as she screams, and I'm trying to gain some control of a run-away truck. Bouncing in the seat doesn't help, then I pop the clutch, and the engine starts, I press on the brakes, and the Truck starts sliding on the dirt, then stops, just before running off the fucking road, with a 500 ft. drop on the side. In a four-wheel drive, I back up and back onto the Tank Road. WOW, here she comes running down this same steep road laughing. She says, "You looked like a cartoon flying past me, honey. Are you ok?" "No," I answer, then reply, "Now let's get you home, sweetheart."

I stopped back at Lumberyard; they had the paperwork done. The Sgt. said, "What happened to your---" I stopped him and said, "Don't ask, bye." Later at FLC, Gunny asked the same thing, "What happened to your windshield?" I said, "A football hit it." He laughed and said, "Ok, LeBeau, if you say so." I replied, "Someday, I will tell you, but not right now. I have to get over to a rifle inspection. Later, Gunny."

Since my rifle was an M-14 w/selector, most Marines at FLC carried M-14s. The job I had with Captain James and

Top Borders was off-base duty, moving all around I Corps', AOR. (Area of Responsibility). It was a weapon of my choice, with attached Bipods.

This was my official job with them, but I did much more. Over the past year, I have survived a year of experience and thus gained a tremendous amount of field experience. Secondly, I fell in love with my weapon and learned everything there was to know about this gorgeous piece of weaponry. My rifle was indeed my best friend, and we had many conversations. The Marine mystic is true. This dam thing is almost a person in many ways and becomes very personal. It was never him; it was always her. I say with life-saving respect. She loves being cleaned, also unique, and caressed. This rifle inspection is like showing her off to others. It also makes me proud of what I have—a well-oiled, clean killing machine, and she's mine. Well used, and signs of the wear and tear that we shared together in our experiences of life-or-death situations. At rife inspections, we stood bolt and told of our kinship. One more reflection, the rifle-sling was reversed, hanging in a port position, for a quick fire from the hip emergency. I also learned from the field of combat that a stable prone position I could lay down some very effective and deadly fire power. I added to her a bipod for accurate firing, for those types of occasions, with her legs spread open, which men love to have from time to time.

At inspection, there was Capt. James, Top Borders, Gunny Campbell and SSgt. Benson. Capt. James looks me over and smiles, and proudly snaps my rifle away through the air, almost levitating to his holding position. Slapping it from right to left hand, inspects it and says, "Has she been good to you, LeBeau?" he asks with a cheeky smile.

I reply, "Yes, Sir, she has." with a great show of nonchalance. He looks at me and says. "Her condition shows me some good love and care, LeBeau." I nod affirmatively, "Yes, sir."

He holds my weapon out, and I snap it back quickly, thru the air, left to right, to my port arms position. Next Top Borders gives me a very stern look and a pleasing grin. Next, Gunny Campbell says, "LeBeau, you look like a grunt dressed-out?" I answer, "Because I feel like a grunt sometimes, Gunny." Gunny replies, "Are you a Grunt LeBeau? I quickly respond, "No, but it depends on the situation Gunny." Gunny, "Hmmm." SSgt. Benson was next. SSgt. Benson, "Do you like me, LeBeau?" I quickly respond, "No, Sargent." Benson, "Why?" I reply, "Because you are so ugly, Sgt." SSgt. Benson, "How ugly am I, LeBeau?" I firmly reply, "You are so ugly. The Marine Corps dog looks better than you do." SSgt. Benson, "Then why are you looking at me like that, Marine?" I reply, "Because looking at your face, I remembered that I have a question, Sgt." SSgt. Benson, "And pray to tell me what is that question?" I said to him, "Looking at your ugly face reminded me that I need your permission to go to the Mtn. Rifle range and practice, Sgt." SSgt. Benson, "if my face reminds you of that, you have my permission to go practice." I replied, "Thank you, SSgt. Benson." SSgt. Benson, "That question could have waited until after inspection, Marine." Everyone laughed up and down the formation, including the whole inspection staff.

The rifle range is a little horseshoe near the 11th Marines on the right side of the hill—only 50 yards deep and about 10 yards wide. The evening is an excellent time to practice because most of the action is in the evening, also at night, so the evening subdued light was useful in my practice. I brought an ammo can full of 7.62 rounds, and I am ready to practice. I have been doing this for quite some time when I'm free to do so. Lately, I've been practicing drops and to the prone position, also firing from the hip. The different target debris is left here by others, so my target setups vary. My eye-hand coordination has improved so much that my accuracy is extremely good at almost any range. My sites from the prone position are preset to 12 to 15 clicks elevation with no wind, 5 to 6 clicks right from the 0 standards, then adjusted for wind, if any cross wind. My shoulder and chin weld has instinctively improved beyond my wildest dreams, a nice, sweet spot. Also, my iron-site picture needs improvement, but I'm still on target for body mass, with a nice tight group of holes in the black. This practice had already proved invaluable in the field when I needed it, which could be anytime, anywhere, in all conditions.

My confidence has grown over time. I've been practicing for over an hour when a Jeep pulls up behind me, dust flying. This Marine gets out and walks over to the pistol range, and he also has a 30 Cal. Carbine. I have seen him around before at FLC. Marine? Yes, but Vietnamese, with tight tiger camo trousers, he has a dark Green Beret cover with a Marine emblem pinned on it. The rank is Maj., rough-looking young face with a thin mustache. I noticed that he is a pretty good shot with both weapons. After about 30 mins, he and I have a sit-down on some stacked sandbags.

His English is quite good. We seemed to have a lot in common apart from the slight desire to be alone sometimes.

He says, "I'm Maj. Chiang and you are, L/Cpl. RC LeBeau? I see you are practicing with an M-14 and 45?"

Yes, sir. You can call me RC, Sir. You look familiar, sir. I've seen you around the FLC Base." I answer, and Maj nods.

"Yes, I work with S-2." RC, "Intel." Maj., "Yes." RC, "Do you come here often?" Maj., "Ya, sometimes, still not enough time, but not like I would like too, RC." RC, "You shoot well, Sir."

"Not as good as you, Marine, LOL. I came up here to see and talk to you, RC." RC, "Really?" RC, "Tell me more."

Maj. "RC, you have been seeing one of our agents in Da Nang and developed a relationship with her, which is fine. But my question is, has she ever talked to you about the war?" RC, "No, sir. Not at all."

"She is a double agent and has a VC boyfriend. Did you know that she has a Vietnamese boyfriend? RC, "No, I had no idea." Maj., "Are you sure?" RC, "Yes, sir." Maj., "Good." RC, "I'll stop seeing her then, sir." Maj., "That won't be necessary, RC. We have been watching the two of you for some time." RC, "I've seen her from time to time at the Bazaar." Maj., "We set her up at that Bazaar, and her contact for the local VC was the blind Vietnamese guy who plays a Tính-Tầu. He listens to everything. He recently warned her that he heard the local VC units were planning something big during the TET holiday. He was afraid for her, and he wanted her to go to her boyfriend for safety. RC, "Really." Maj., "She met him at a coffee shop in Da Nang, and he threatened her family. She got scared and left him. Returning home, she was stopped on her way home by one of our plainclothes agents following her on his motorbike. Now I'm telling you all this for a reason." RC, "Why is that?" Maj., "She had found out that the 2nd NVA Division in the Que Son Mountains was planning to attack Da Nang city and Airbase. She is afraid that we will lose this battle and that they will kill her and her family in the battle." RC, "How can I help?" Maj., "She trusts you, and we cannot risk any more contact with her. We also know about yesterday on Freedom hill. RC, "What." We had eyes on her, not you at the top of the hill, a 50 Cal. Machinegun was trying to kill both of you. We believe they were trying to take her out from a mile away. We were zeroing in on that gun location. While the two of you were going down the hill, the sniper had left. But we did get him in the valley.

"Wow," I responded with uncertainty.

"We were on the opposite hill north of your location, glassing the area," Maj said, but I was still not convinced.

"What does all this involve me and your surprise visit with me?" "Because she loves you and trusts you, we need to get a message to her, that's it. Will you help us help her?"

, "I'm a Marine that must answer to my commanders. This stuff is, needed to know shit, and they need to know."

"I will take care of that. Are you in or not.?"

"Ok."

"We'll be in touch." I salute him as he leaves. I'm thinking now what.

What comes after this?

What do I do next?

What happens next?

Do I go back to her, or do I not? These are questions that still need to be answered.

Chapter 3

The Day TET Offensive starts Da Nang

Tuesday, January 30th, 1968,

One day to go…

The Chinese New Year TET has turned into a war. The day that was supposed to be happy. The day that was supposed to be celebrated was turned into a day of war and bloodshed.

Where I was, the thing hadn't changed much. Around here, everything seems normal, but it isn't. The Base is humming like normal, and the bad News. Most of the Vietnamese military standby, 3rd Battalion, and 7th Marines have occupied 2/5 in An-Hoa Combat Base with two companies of 3/7 covering an extended area of 3/5 south of Da Nang at least. That is what I hear. The sound of the military coming in.

I felt like I needed to go to the Lumberyard. When Gunny surprisingly comes up to me and tells me, "Hey LeBeau, I need you to go to the Lumberyard." I say, "Sure, Gunny." Gunny also told me the PC was in use, and I would have to grab the big duce and half, Truck. He explained that the inventory sheets were incomplete and they would have to re-submit them today. That means hanging out at the Lumberyard. I went S-2 to see the Vietnamese Major. Upon arrival, the Major was expecting me. The cleric announced me, and I went into his office. He said, "At ease, RC. "Just as I was going to tell him about what Gunny said, he stopped me. Maj. "RC I made Capt. James knows the situation and is on board with my need to use you today. Gunny arranged the reason to leave the Base and go to the Lumberyard. RC "That's why the big Truck, sir?

"Maj., "You're going to bring her and her family back here. A-SAP. After, we will be leaving a team there to welcome her VC boyfriend and his friends at their house. The team will not enter the house until you leave with the family. Then we will chop H-34 her out to a C 130 plane, flying her and her family to the Philippines. There, they will be safe and sound." RC, WOW, that sounds great, sir." Maj., "We take care of our own. There will be no place safe for her in Vietnam or for her or her family." RC, "Some buddy may compromise the family if they find out they are going to the Philippines, sir." Maj. "No, we told her and her family that we have a big house in Saigon and showed them pictures. I'm telling you this because if you two love birds want to see each other, maybe after the war, she now thinks it will be Saigon. The address and all. You, on the other hand, now know the secret destination. Just reverse the street number 4657, and use 12th street, with Manila,

Philippines. We think she will write that down for you to find her in Saigon. Please don't blow it, RC; we will tell her that on her flight." RC, "You can count on me, sir. Thank you for letting me do this for her and her family." Maj., "If this information is true, she has saved many lives. If it is not true, we have at least saved her and her families lives, and we still get her boyfriend and his friends." It's a win for all of us. Dismissed, Marine." RC, "Yes, Sir."

After leaving the meeting, I got the Truck. I felt a certain calmness in the air with the arrangement. The action wasn't taking place on my route there. Going to the Lumberyard was not a problem. The drive to the house was going to be uneventful, maybe. The people were tense, looking like someone was hiding something. I went straight to the Lumberyard using the back road next to Hill 268. When I arrived, I told the staff Sgt. at the Lumberyard to ensure everyone there was always wearing full combat gear and on for the next week. That shit was hitting the fan. Then we both laughed since this place was not a very defendable place to be, and neither was the Pass up the road. I gave him the papers and got a cup of coffee at their makeshift Mess. SSgt. Came out of the BLQ and asked, "Are you spending the night? And why the big Truck.? My answer was, "No, they had me doing some other things, and that we would be here tomorrow to pick up the paperwork, and seriously, full combat on everyone here.

"SSgt., "Ok, Ok, thanks for the heads up. RC" "Everybody seems to be a little tense about this Holiday."

The Sgt., amused at that revelation, smiled. I also mentioned for him to keep the boom, boom girls, out of the compound, at least until he leaves.

He laughed at me or maybe at my audacity to talk about the boom-boom girls at the time of war.

Then I went on my way to my lady's house.

The road to her place was uneventful. With III MAF just down the road where I was turning, there seemed to be a lot of activity. The information was that NVA /VC had moved out of the hills west of Hill 327 Quang Nam providence meaning a significant offensive and big push had already begun. Arriving there seemed less welcoming than before, but maybe the big Truck had surprised them at her house.

I noticed a lot of Vietnamese militaries up and down the street. They were patrolling the pathway, or maybe they were keeping an eye on us. Since I had full combat gear on, with my soft cover, I had left my Helmet in the Truck seat. She greeted me and handed me a note, which I stuck in my jungle fatigues' top breast pocket. Then parked the back of the Truck in front of the house.

After about 2 hours of them loading the Truck with stuff, it was time to loan her and the family. With all the action going on in the Da Nang area, I felt the way back to my Base was the same way I had come there and used the back gate to the Base as my entry point. It was getting late, and darkness was my enemy's friend. I put her grandmother in the front seat with her mother. Everyone else had to ride in the back with their stuff. So as not to flag the enemy, I had them close the curtain on the back of the Truck. The ladies in the front with me told them not to wear their lamp shade hats.

As I traveled back to Base, I stopped at the Lumberyard and picked up the paperwork, and told the Sgt. that TOP might be evacuating the Lumberyard. If he does, I will be back to pick you Marines up for safety's sake. The Sgt. said, "It will be dark by then." I reply, "If I don't come back in three hours, I'm not coming later, Sgt."

When I arrived at the rear gate of my Base, the Marines were ready to lock it down. I then left and followed the perimeter road around to the Command offices, which were surprisingly busy. The sun was setting, and I left the Truck at the Command road entrance. I was walking and saluting on my way to S-2. The Maj. introduced me to a LtCol. Singlabb of SOG, who was wearing Tiger bar-jungle fatigues, after a stern salute, the LtCol. said to me, "Do you have a package for me?" RC., "Yes, I do, sir. in the Truck to my rear, sir." The LtCol.

He tells me, "RC, take that Truck to the Helipad and wait for the chopper to arrive for the pickup. Please have our guests wait outside of the Truck. A Chopper will be there in an hour. I will have drinks and snacks delivered to them A-SAP from our Mess Truck while they wait for their ride." RC, "Yes, right away, Sir." LtCol., "You did a good job, RC, and I won't forget this. Good job, Marine; now get out of here." I saluted them, did an about-faced, went to the Truck, and took the family to the base Helipad. The Helipad, used by the Airbourne Division, had moved northward off base. It took two H-34s for the dust-off, one for the family's stuff and one for the family. They were all crying as I waved them off. I watched them fly over Da Nang Bay until I lost sight of the choppers in the darkness of the bay.

From there, I Tripped over to the NCO quarters near the Officers' Quarters. I saw SSgt. Benson asked him where Gunny and MSgt. Borders were at, and he directed me to his BLQ. I knocked on his screen door and shouted, "TOP" He shared with Gunny, and Top came to the door. Top asked, "What's up, LeBeau? I asked, "Top, I know it is getting late, but those Marines at the Lumberyard would like to know if you want them to evacuate the yard with everything happening around us?" Top, "What do you think, RC?" RC, "Well, if it were my call, I would go get them because I would hate to have them on my conscious if something happened to them. Top." Top, "LeBeau, you're going to make Corporal yet. Good Idea, RC. Get them, and we'll prepare them in our NCO, BLQs if necessary. Gunny, do we have room for that SSgt.?" Gunny, "Yes, we can do that." Top, "Then I'll take care of the rest. And LeBeau, don't get yourself in the process killed." RC, "You got it, TOP. And thanks, Gunny."

I hopped into the Truck, brought the Marines back from the Lumberyard, and finally got some shuteye.

Chapter 4

The TET Battle Begins Tonight

This night, before I went to my Rack, I knew the next morning was going to be more ferocious, and it was going to last a lot longer, and maybe it would be remembered for a long.

And that's what happened.

Alert I woke up early this Wednesday morning, January 31, 1968. The day the first phase of the assault began when NVA/VC forces were getting ready to simultaneously attack a number of targets around Vietnam.

Daybreak, three S's (shit, shower, shave), then to the Chow Hall or Mess Hall for breakfast. On my way to the supply office, I ran into a Marine from our K-9 unit working with his Dog. As I walk up to him, I say, "Beautiful German Shepard Marine. What's his name? The Marine replies, "Bullet." I reply, "Great name, Bullet," and his Dog perks his ears up at the mere mention of his name. "I love dogs. Later Marine." He replies, "Later."

Arriving at the office, Marines are still coming for work. I ask, "Where is Gunny?" These Marines are my friends and also from my BLQ and squad. Their names are Camden, and Castle, which was with me last week when we got ambushed. Camden, "They are all at a meeting and will be here around 0800. Then we all have a meeting with them." RC, "What's going on?" Castle, "Apparently, An-Hoa is rotating with the absence of 2/5 Marines forwarded to Phu Bai and 3/7 Marines filling in at An-Hoa. That is why you and the Lt. are not going to An-Hoa. With the current situation in the field, things are changing rapidly everywhere." RC, "I see." Camden says, "RC, did you go to the Lumberyard yesterday? RC, "Ya." Camden, "Who has the inventory sheet? RC, "Gunny." Camden, "Company G, from 2/7, will patrol the Nam-O area tonight. I saw them at the Mess Hall last night and this morning. They told me a big attack is likely." RC," Ya well, a company of Marines is nobody to be fucking with when it comes to that."

Tonight's Brief

Gunny and everyone in our Command showed up in the office. They just looked at us and seemed to be worried or had a concerned demeanor about themselves. Gunny, "Here is what's up. A large NVA/VC is moving in the direction of Da Nang and our direction, so pass the word. Also, since the VC has spies on this Base, all indigenous Vietnamese personnel are to stay home until further notice. This alert is still in place and has become immediate as of tonight. The III MAF has reported that scattered and intermittent attacks throughout the Da Nang area will probably occur tonight, with mortars and rocket attacks. We had little or no warnings during previous rocket attacks on this Base. As you know, Company G of 2/7 Marines will be patrolling the area north of us around the Nam-O village and Bridge crossing the Cu De river. The Clutch platoon will have a perimeter watch, with two squads on standby at the guard shack near the CP Bunker across the street. RC, your fire team will be at the guard shack, Sgt. Ski is your squad leader tonight— your task, along with Sgt. Ski is to protect the CP bunker at all costs. Understood? And Sgt. Ski has already told." The rest of the Platoon is to be at the northern Perimeter bunkers. I want everyone to be in place by 20:00. That's it, now get back to work." I asked Gunny about the An-Hoa trip with the Lt., and he told me that because of enemy activity, for now, it has been postponed, but still a priority; he didn't know when.

Not to telegraph Company G's movements, they have been moving elements in covered Trucks all day. Moving a Marine Company was no small task. It was interesting how they did that movement. Squads were in warehouses, loading trucks with their equipment and Marines. Then, they left the Base back gate, headed toward Da Nang, and later reversed course somewhere online in Da Nang and headed back to Nam-O north on highway 1. It wasn't even noticeable for me to know what they were doing. But it was a full-day maneuver, quite ingenious. By nightfall, they had seeded the entire Nam-O area.

The Base Rocket Attack

When I arrived at the Guard Shack, it was empty. About 12 empty foldup Cots opened and laded out in order with sleeping gear on each one. I was fully loaded, with about 35 to 40 pounds of gear, not including my rifle. I was bored, unsaddled everything, and fixed my rack. This room filled up soon with the rest of the squad. After a few hours, everyone left for the CP Bunker including me. Every night at about 22:00, the 11th Marine battery had assigned areas for flare drops over certain regions; we also put out patrols for LPs and reactionary responses. All our bunkers had intruder alert systems with night vision on the north side of Red Beach or FLC's Base. The Base was lights out tonight, and all vehicles used night light shields while traveling around the Base. Red streams fell from the sky, raining down on distant targets, with ground flashes and very faint rumblings. Shortly before midnight, I returned to the shack, laid down, and slept, bored and tired.

Suddenly, waking me from a dead sleep, big booms were hitting our Base. The Siren across the street started to whale. We were under attack, and I reached for my gear in the flashing light. Still waking up, I was stumbling and fumbling, trying to get my shit together. Three Marines in the room yelled at me, get to the CP bunker, see you there, RC. I was left alone in the room with dangling flares providing a waving light in the room. I looked back at my rack to ensure I have everything and rush to the door. A rocket hitting so close to the shack the sound was deafening; as soon as I opened the screen door, another rocket hit close by with its thunderous boom. I think, fuck that was close in behind the shack in a stockpile to my right.

I stopped, looked in the air, and heard the rocket engine stop, with what looked like a telephone pole sailing in the air and landing farther down range on the Base with another big boom. Those 122 rockets are big boomers and are still coming in. Moving to my left to cross the road. I glance off over my shoulder to my right. This 122 is hitting right behind a steel Conex Box. Witnessing the flash and the boom instantly, the blast surrounded my body. In a split second, I could feel the shock wave's pressure engulfing me, which knocked me down to the ground. I have no idea if I was dead or alive. After that, I felt like I was waking up again from an absolute nightmare. I could barely hear the Siren across the street, rolling on my back. I could see another rocket flying in the air high above me. My ears are gone, and rolling back to my knees. I started checking out to see if I'd been hit or bleeding. Breathing heavily, I think I'm ok. Kneeling, I gather my gear I crouch to a stand up position, looking at the black mangled Conex Box torn to shreds, and smoldering. I say to myself, Holy Fuck, that box just saved my life. My ears felt fully plugged, and I moved my jaw to see if I could clear them, but no help, still blocked. As I looked across the street, I noticed tracer rounds passing down the road from my left.

I instinctively know that every fifth round is a tracer. I also noticed that the rounds stopped, when the flare had stopped and burned out. So, I waited to run across the open area street until another flare burned out. Still deaf but recovering, now I see my opportunity to run obliquely. I get to the middle of the street, a flare pops its light, and rounds begin coming down the road again. I stopped as more bullets were flying all around me. The flare burns out. I run again for cover and rechecked myself. My right leg was in pain at the kneecap. I take all my gear off, examine everything and notice shrapnel in the back of my flak Jacket, but no penetration just burned rips. This is so fucked up, but now I must get to the CP bunker.

As I get to the Command Bunker, when Sgt Ski yells for me to get on the roof of the Command Bunker, then Sgt. Ramirez saw me limping and helped me up the sandbags to the Bunker's top. It gave a commanding view of the battle around us, with tracers flying everywhere. I was exhausted by the adrenaline of the moment. I found myself collecting myself, like a boxer sitting on his stool, after a few rounds of boxing. Everyone was talking, but I wasn't lessening to a word they were saying. As I was still recovering, I saw the Da Nang Airbase was getting hit. Also, not far from us, the 11th Marines were hit.

After an hour, Ramirez told me to go to Sickbay in front of CP Bunker and have my leg examined. I said, "That I was ok," and he insisted. I climbed down from the CP bunker and went in their back door. A Corpsmen looked at me and asked, "What is wrong with you?" I told him my leg was bothering me. He told me to sit down over there and that he would be with me in a moment. I looked around and said, "That's ok. I'll come back later." He said sternly, "No, I insist you stay here and wait." I felt guilty because they were so many wounded and everyone was so busy and I could still walk, but I waited. Then I could tell the wetness in my boot was blood draining down my leg. I said to myself, hmmm, I'm going to take my boot off.

When I did, it revealed my blood-soaked sock. I saw the tear in my trousers but not much blood there. The blood on my sock was starting to harden, so I limped over to a sink and started to rinse my foot and sock. With a blue surgical cap on, a Doc walked by and looked at me and my foot. He smiled and said, "Looks like we will have to take your foot off, Marine." Chuckling he walked off to tend to more meaningful work in the ER. I looked at my bloodied foot and smiled at his sense of humor. The white returned to my sock, kind of pinkish. Then I used my foot-sock to clean my bloodied foot.

After all this, I returned to the seating area. About ten minutes later, the Corpsman returned. He examined my leg, cleaned it with some stinging stuff, put butterfly stickers on to close the wound, and covered it with gauze and tape. He said, "Here is some extra gauze but don't get it too wet, and don't remove the butterflies for at least a week, ok? I replied, "ok, thanks a lot." The Corpsman replied, "I have to go and remove another Marine's foot." We both laughed. Corpsman, "We also have a sense of humor around here." I said, "Then Doc told you, huh?" He smiled and left.

Upon returning to the Command Post bunker, Sgt. Ski said, "RC. Are you ok? I said, "Ya." to Sgt. Ski, "Grab these ammo cans and let's bring them up the street to the west perimeter fighting hole." Skirting the Quonset huts and buildings as we went up to the foxhole. There I noticed a small Vietnamese shack white cement house outside the fence line. To the right down the fence line road was a towering bunker looking over a rice field on the other side of the cyclone fence. I asked these Marines if anyone was in that house. One of the Marines said, "Don't know, over an hour ago, we received automatic fire from there for about ten minutes, then silence. I think they were using an M-60 machine gun. Tell tail Red tracers, huh" Ski asked, "How is your ammo? A Marine answered, "Fine, we had the house in a crossfire. Between that Bunker and us over there, we chewed that house up. The fire was coming from below those widows. They may have had a trench under the ground at the bottom of that house wall, below those windows. They may have survived the crossfire. Too far for us to throw a grenade, but an M-79 grenade launcher would do the trick. I think they Dee-dee out of here myself, but we won't know until there is a morning sweep through this area."

Returning to the CP bunker, we got word that an assault of Da Nang city was taking place, near Marble Mtn., southeast around the Cau Dau river from Vien Dien river, and the Airbase were also engaged. Our Base was on full alert, and CP Commanders briefed us that there was at least a Battalion of NVA/VC (because the NVA had intertwined the VC with 60% NVA and 40% VC units) this Battalion engaged with Company G of 2/7 Marines south of the Hai Van Pass and fighting alongside Allied defenses. The 2nd VC Sapper Battalion had blown three bridges on the south approach of the Pass. That would make two enemy Battalions, and the Nam O bridge on Hwy. 1 was still secure. Fighting in and around Nam O lasted well into the morning. They also informed me that an VC flag was posted just outside our northern perimeter, about two clicks out.

The next Day, February 1st, 1968

The 2/7 Marines were tied up north of the river with action south of Pass along Hwy 1.

The ARVN 5th Ranger Battalion moved up Hwy 1 to the left and right side of the FLC Base. They engaged the enemy VC/NVA that planted that flag north of us. Then we witnessed the Air and artillery support in the din of the morning again the VC/NVA positions. We watched the Vietnamese Rangers assault the village of Nam O. The villagers were hiding in their few shelters, afraid for their lives while the action continued.

A few hours later, a crowd of Vietnamese civilians came out of the village of Nam O on Hwy 1 a crowd of village people moving south, and the VC were mixed in with them, attacking the CAP Q4. The civilians were crying and afraid, the VC mixed with them were determined to get rid of us. The VC were using the civilian's fear as human shields moving towards us used them to hide their presents.

The VC was using these people as human shields were cowards. With women and children carrying VC flags, the VC fired from behind them. We saw CAP Marines and PFs shooting the armed VC with accurate shots, thus dispersing the crowd and exposing the enemy. It was sick to watch. The villagers running to our Base, they scattered these people many gathering in the white sand and lying down along our northeast perimeter. We could only pick off the enemy if they were the only ones carrying a weapon. We were desperately trying not to shoot any innocent people. That is where accurate Marine rifle fire comes into play.

Small enemy people make small targets and are extremely difficult to hit. Surprisingly, out of over 500 Vietnamese village people, all the VC were killed, later we counted over 50 enemies killed, with 11 civilians dead and over 60 civilians wounded. Out of all those people, we felt like crying but also felt blessed at the same time. Welcome to February 1st.. It was so fucked up. None of us could eat or sleep most of the day when the fighting stopped around us, but still, battles were going on in the village of Nam O, the war continued. Beyond our sight, the carnage continues all around the Da Nang area on this day. We streamed out the gate to help as much as we could. With a pallet of body bags, bodies started to pile up. The Medical Corpsmen treated the wounded, marking enemy body bags with a black Magicmarker, VC. It was a fucking mess.

Fighting was still going on, and it felt like a time-loop. There was a time when I thought I was living the same day over and over again.

The same day that lasted for a lifetime. The fight just wouldn't end. As the fight went on, we tried to keep Hwy 1 open as reinforcements went into the fray down HWY. 1 and dispersed into the battle zone.

Errant rounds from the battle in Nam O were still causing casualties all around us as we worked with the people in a daze wandering around, stunned and shocked. We saw people on the ground. The blood on the roads started to smell that familiar smell that I knew so well, that you will never forget. One black tooth lady, crying, ran over to me, her body hitting me, knocked off my Helmet, and then kicked, spitting at the body I was loading into the body bag. She screamed at the body, "VC., number 10 thou." As she assaulted the body, I yelled, "Mark this one as VC." I walked her over to a Corpsman to look at her arm, which was bleeding. I was already bloody everywhere, and then she hugged me again, adding more blood to me. I looked at her, and she smiled then dropping, as she collapsed to the ground. The Corpsman rushed to her and said, "She has lost a lot of blood. I'll do what I can to save her life, Marine. Thanks." He put a tourniquet on her arm from her torn shirt sleeve to stop the bleeding. There was nothing more he could do for her.

Suddenly, a VC fired a B-40 rocket at us from a village building. It exploded in the garbage dump across the street from where we were, and no one was injured. A marine down the road dispatched that VC hiding by that building. After a few hours, we went back to our Base. I went directly to the crowded showers. The water was cold as ice, but I didn't give a shit, and neither did anyone else. Suddenly, the Base siren started whaling, but I stayed, and so did everyone else. It turned out to be a false alarm. No rockets or mortars, "No incoming." someone yelled into the shower room.

Now over twenty-four hours of very little sleep, clean and refreshed after an hour of cleaning my body and gear, lying on my rack, with my clean T-Shirt and skives on, my mind is drifting. Suddenly, and surprisingly awakening as time had passed like a minute which was hours. I could hear the rumblings of the battle still going on in the distance of Nam O. Hungry for food and information, I ate and went to the Command Post bunker. I gathered information from as many knowing people as I could find that had Intel of the war.

Late February 1, I found out that the city of Da Nang was still engaged, along with the surrounding area of the Da Nang TAOR. The NVA and VC seemed to retreat, but the main force was still moving in the An-Hoa area an around Dodge city, so named because of all shootem ups in that area. They believed the NVA's 2nd Division was still trying to take down the city of Da Nang and the airport as this NVA 2nd Division was slowly moving into position. What has been happening so far in our northern area points to this being a diversionary attraction of small engagements to draw us away from their main movement of approach to the Da Nang area from the southwest Que Son mountains and Tam Khe. Thus, it trickles into the combat area, with reconstruction and assembly for a more significant force. If this were true, they would hit in strength from the south of Da Nang, with another limited attraction here in the north of Da Nang. All this, they estimated, would happen over a week. Of course, this was an educated guess on our part, and the commanders are planning accordingly for their reaction. Logistically it sounded right because, with troops, you need equipment to be moved and carried by hand. Across the countryside, not by roads and crossing rivers.

In my mind, I'm going, the VC/NVA have a big Logistical problem to accomplish that type of a move. Wow.

Chapter 5
February 2 to February 5

As time moved on, everything changed, but we didn't. It's not like we didn't try. We did; we tried to change. Because if we stick to the pain — we can't live, and we wouldn't be able to move on.

And we must move on ... let it go. Or else the pain would consume us. The most absurd part is it worked. Because along the war scenes, along with the pain and the death around me, I had somehow managed to extricate myself from this pit of anger.

For the next few days, there hasn't been much action in the immediate area around Red Beach, FLC was still getting Rocket attacks from time to time at night. But it was nothing like what we had witnessed.

I got word that I was going to the An-Hoa combat base by the river and coal mines on February 6. During this time, everything was going to be shipped by choppers, but compared to the first two days, there was a lull around most of the Da Nang sector. All the bases in this sector were getting hit, and it was in the wee hours. The Airbase and the Ammo dump by hill 327 rockets hit. The enemy pushes on Da Nang, not finished yet. One time the Airfield was hit with over 30 122 Rockets, destroying aircraft and an empty, newly constructed building on the SW side of the Airfield. Since the Korean Marines in the Hoi-An were still engaged, the commanders hinted and speculated that this action was shadowing the VC and NVA main force infiltrating the south. The groups formed at predetermined rally points south of the Cau-Do River. To confirm this idea, my commander and Marine intelligence said that the NVA 2nd Division had moved to the Go-Noi Island, not far from An-Hoa and Hill 55. He informed me that an H-34 would take us there. Also, it would have to fly over 5,000 ft to avoid enemy contact.

I don't know how long we will be there in An-Hoa. Everything in Happy Valley is every Base seems to have been hit with mortars or rockets. Heavy action has started in the Hue area, including Saigon. The ebb and flow of enemy movements to our south are visible at night but far enough away that the booms are distant to our ears. Tomorrow we will be picked up here for our flight to An-Hoa.

There has been little to no action over the past few days here on our Base, but we couldn't let our guard down. The combat action was more intense to the south of Da Nang, out of our sight and ears. As of February 5, this action involves the ROK Marines, ARVNs, 3/5 Marines, and 11th Marines artillery trying to keep the Rocket belt around Da Nang secure and air support.

We were sleeping in our BLQ bunkers again tonight when around 01:30, rockets were coming into our area. So much for our needed rest. Our eyes were closed, but our minds were on complete alert, so the hoax rest was the only rest we could get. And, at this time, I would take sleep that I could get. The lieutenant was in our fighting hole of our Bunker, watching the 122mm rockets coming in along with enemy mortars hitting outside our base. His radio said that the 1st Cavalry helipad outside the wire got mortared, and there were casualties. Inside the Village of Nam O, more likely the mortaring was coming from there. The radio said that our Base helipad was not hit, though.

The 11th Marines counter fire had silenced everything by 04:00 that morning of February 6. In the early morning darkness, we were still on alert.

An-Hoa

The chopper loaded up with the supplies that were needed on two other Marine choppers. Our birds headed immediately over the Da Nang Bay. We were mountain high as we passed over Marble Mountain and headed southwest to An-Hoa.

While flying over the battled areas, there were little signs of conflict on the ground, and numerous craters were visible, scattered here, there, and everywhere. We could not reflect on whether the Craters were past or present in the rice paddies' squares. As we passed some high country, the pilot yelled to us that we were receiving some ground small arms fire as we approached the An-Hoa area. As we landed on the An-Hoa airstrip, the Lieutenant went to the Base Headquarters (HQ) office and for me to meet him back at this location at 18:00. I saluted him and walked around the Base, which was pretty quiet now. A big C-130 landed on the runway, spraying a light mist in the rain, billowing in the air around its landing.

On the south end of the Base facing some distant hills, I sat on some sandbags of a fighting hole, gazing over the south perimeter spans from left to right—there was a familiar smell in the air of death, rotting flesh, and blood. Even after a rain, that smell tells you that you just entered a battlefield. The scent permeates everything it touches until the rot has the rains wash it away. Those who visit these types of areas feel it is a smell that is incomparable to any other. This smell you know will be recognized your whole lifetime. If you smell it again, you will immediately understand what it is. "Death."

The skies are overcast, and where my mind is at right now, the silence was so much I could acutely hear a Marine approaching me from the rear, still away. Not even a bug could sneak up on me with my mind where it is now.

As this Marine gets closer, without turning to see him, I say to him, "What's up, Marine?" Then I turned to look at him. He was a lean young man with nervous hands and an excited look.

He bubbles up with wry amusement; I sensed that he looked relieved to have someone to talk t. "Hey." He responded. Imminent, he finds himself a place to sit and says nothing. A few minutes pass, and he says, "I noticed you from my Bunkers guard post and decided to join you, "Sir."

In the Vietnam field, many officers didn't wear their rank or under their gear or clothing. So, because everyone in their unit knows who their officers are, unmarked and uncertain, Marines sometimes would address even a private as "Sir." Since this Marine did not see any rank, he ended the sentence with a "Sir." Since my rank was hidden under my combat gear, he had no choice but to end his statement with a "Sir." Replacement second lieutenants in the field, Marines often reminded the 2nd Lieutenants. by Marines around them with, Sir, your gold bars are going to draw fire, Sir." I turned to this Marine smiling and said, "I'm not an officer Marine." Then he smiled back. "So, what's up, Marine?" Since I was 21 yrs. old, and most Marines were 18 or 19 yrs. old, I could see why a mistake like this would happen.

After spending some time on the perimeter talking to this Marine, I grabbed some food at the Mess Hall and ate outside with some other Marines. By doing this, I found out that over time, I could get vital information on the users of our supplies that are being sent to them and listen to their bitches and complaints. Then I would convey that information to my commanders for evaluation of priorities of supply items shipped to different locations. Since these Marines don't know I'm doing that, they are very open about things that they are telling me. More so than even their commanders hear, since rightfully so, their commanders are very strict with more important things on their minds, and supply infractions are not one of them. So vital information can be gathered with my sit-downs with Marines at different bases I had to go to. My commanders have realized my importance in the field and not at a desk in some office. In my entire tour in Vietnam, I have had a great relationship with all the commands I went to because of my no-bullshit attitude about things I saw. That is why the new Lieutenant turned me loose as soon as we landed.

My Logistical expert training mentioned the importance of feet in the supply chain. This is one of the most essential items a Marine can have besides his rifle, water, food, and lodging. In any environment, your feet are one of the most important. As I wondered about these combat bases. Marines coming in from the field of operation, I'm always was looking at their feet. I look at their clothing condition, the wear and tear of their gear, the shape of their weapons, and now most Marines would sport two canteens of water, and pouches, ripped or torn holding them. All that, but their feet. The way they walk tells me that their feet are hurting. Socks, if they are wearing any are in good condition. These are the reasons why I would go on patrol with them. Without the proper footwear, these Marines' morale will be low, grumpy, and not as effective as they should be in saving the lives of other Marines. That is how important their feet are.

In a Jungle environment, even more so, the feet are essential. Many good Marine commanders are aware of this. In non-contested moments is an excellent time to do 50/50-foot inspections in the field of a combat environment. NDP (Night Defensive Positions) Just 30 minutes or less, 1/3 of the Marine unit can inspect, 1/3 of the Marines feet and 1/3 checks the third and so on, during R&R in the field. At least a one-foot inspection would be for back-and-forth patrols of 5 to 10 miles in all environments. I noticed some Marines thought it was funny when they removed their socks and boots during a river crossing, which is a big no-no. They believe they are cool, but they can be wrote-up for that. However, commanders must do a dry-out after crossing if conditions and time allow for it. Leeches are another good reason to inspect the body.

At An-Hoa, everything on these Marines is in order, with only a few infractions. But we were still waiting for returning patrols that had some firefights during their watch. The 3/7th Marines platoon on Hill 65 will rotate in and out of An-Hoa soon. The meeting with the Lieutenant was on time, and he informed me that we would spend the night there. This Lieutenant was only one year older than me, so we got along famously. The difference between these new second lieutenants and grunt second lieutenants was that new second lieutenants were always trying to prove something but were still humble to NCOs. In the field of combat, since the 2nd Lieutenants had a high rate of being hit in battle so they always listened to their NCO's suggestions or direction for their command.

This night at An-Hoa was no different than other stays I had experienced here.

I found an available rack next to the Airfield, and with the open view to the north, I could witness the hot war going on around Happy Valley, hills 37, 55, and other locations dotted around this field of battle. At night this display is spectacular but deadly.

I helped the Lieutenant with the logistical tasks. The Marines had moved outside the wire before dawn, but the Base was relatively busy. I picked a late breakfast before they closed and had a good night's sleep, which I hadn't had in a long time. Food, and sleep, energized me. Later that afternoon, the Lieutenant informed me that he would not be staying there and flying me back to my Base. He didn't know when that would be. He told me to gear up and be ready at a moment's notice. Later an H-146 showed up. When the crew offloaded the gear from the chopper, it would be off to my Base, which is what I thought. The night sight of the area showed flares everywhere and red and white tracers flying back and forth on the ground at different locations. I was right next to the door watching this wartime spectacle. I could hear pings on the chopper skin but no penetration that I could tell.

We landed on the tarmac at the Da Nang airbase, and the Base was blacked out everywhere. I asked the pilot if I should stay on board. He asked, where was I going? And I said, FLC. He said, You on your own, Marine. Checking for information, I found out Hwy one was closed due to enemy activity. Great I thought, then it dawned on me that Dennis Hammond's compound was just south on Hwy 1 near the Airbase base. I when to the north gate near Hwy 1 and figured I would spend the night there. Base police let me through with a warning of enemy activity in that area. He wanted to know where I was going, and I answered the CAP unit by the Bridge next to Hwy 1 . He said put your Helmet on and lock and load your weapon, Marine. It is still early evening, but it is still fluid with enemy activity all around the airbase. I answered, "Roger that...."

Chapter 6

February 7th & 8th to Echo-4

Heading south on Hwy 1, all the shops are locked down and quiet. Darker than I have ever seen it. Passing occupied Airbase bunkers on the other side of their wire, I felt vulnerable and alone, which was not a good feeling. I could hear them talking as I walked down the road, some snickers and laughing coming from the bunkers to my left that I chose to ignore. Entering the Hoa Vang village by the site of empty shell casings lying around and damage, it was apparent some heavy fighting had taken place around here. My inner alert was entering my brain. I could see the ornamental entrance of the Bridge way ahead of me. I felt for the first time on this highway that I might be entering enemy territory. Distant flares were in the sky, silence, no dogs barking. It felt kind of weird and imposing.

The ammo dump was dark off to the left of freedom hill, with flares popping a swing lightly in the sky. As I got closer to the Bridge, I could feel weapons pointing at me. Then I stopped in the middle of the road and yelled, "Marine approaching." I heard some Vietnamese language talking, and I thought, I'm fucked. Is it the enemy or ARVNs? Then there was English, an American voice said, advance Marine to be recognized. The lights were on me, and I put my hands up. A voice yells, keep coming, keep coming. Then I put my hands down, I said, "thank God for you being here, Marine I heard Vietnamese talking and to myself I said holy fuck, I'm done for." The Marine laughs

After crossing this familiar Cam Le bridge, I stopped and asked this ARVN which way to the CAP unit near Lo Giang. His heavy accent indicated that enemy activity was everywhere and that it would not be safe to go to Lo Giang. Striking a conversation with other ARVNs, I discovered that the action has been quite heavy the past few days , and everyone was on full alert. I went to this Marine that had a box of small explosives and was detonating them in the water by the Bridge. This was to keep enemy divers from blowing up the Bridge. Through casual conversation, I learned that Lo Giang villagers used a well-beaten path that obliquely went east along the Cau Do River, then headed southeast to the Village, and that the CAP unit was along that path. He said between here and there at night would be very dangerous, but if a patrol was going that way to use them but he doubted it. But you would be stupid to do that on your own. As I scanned the area around Da Nang, the river action was just about everywhere, with lots of flares at different locations. I decided to stay there for the night and pick it up in the morning to go to the Lo Giang CAP. I found a spot next to a sandbagged placement and slept. The noise far away, kept waking me up many times. Being on the south end of the Bridge, the noise was louder and close. Off to my left, I could see flashes and muffled explosions where I had intended to go. I summarized that if the CAP unit was not getting hit—the clatter of small arms fire mixed into the blasts was not in that area. As I looked around, I saw everyone at the Bridge was hunkered down.

A squad of Marines crossed the Bridge on the south side, followed by a team of ARVNs. Redeveloping other defensive positions on the Bridge approach along Highway 1. I put my bipods out, positioned myself on the path, and then carefully and silently went to the CAP unit compound. About an hour later or more, I was finally at the CAP compound. On my way there, I often hit the dirt, keeping the flares from silhouetting me as I moved slowly down the path. I also felt that I was being watched the closer I got to the compound.

At the gate I asked this Marine where Dennis Hammond was, and he chuckled and said Dennis was at Echo-2 across the river near the Hoa Vang village. I told him I wasn't going to go there now that would be stupid, this Marine said that I was already stupid coming here; I told him that I had a strange feeling of being watched even though I was trying to be as stealthy as possible. He replied, "You were being watched, coming in our kill zone like that once again how stupid you were, we could have killed you on your approach here you dumb ass fucking Marine." In his small talk, he told me about what was happening around them the past few days. He told me to find a place to relax and stay out of everybody's way, wait till morning. I found my niche, took off all my gear, and slept. However, sleep was not in the cards for me though I was in and out of a sleepy state of mind that just didn't work for me. I did not know what was happening around us with a distant sound of choppers. Ambient noise around the camp, there was a chill in the air, making it hard to sleep. I think a few hours had passed because my watch had stopped, and I had no clue what time it was. So, I saddled up and went to a nearby Bunker to see and hear about what was going on. At the Bunker's entrance, I stopped and had a smoke in my cupped hand, underneath the flap of my flak jacket to hide the flash of my lighter. There was still a slight chill in the air, which slightly severed my body. I heard mumbling coming from inside the Bunker.

The watch Marine hardly noticed my entrance as he was on the field phone. He mumbled his name here, and I replied, "RC here," and said, "Boring, huh." He replied, "Ya, there seems to be a lot of activity happening a couple of miles southwest of us here." Then he said, "The Ville is strange tonight; the lack of natural bug noises reminds me of a few nights ago when they attacked the airbase across the river northeast of here. There was a lot of action there.". I replied, "Sounds spooky." A marine on the Cot said, "Hey, pipe down." We shut up. The Marine I was talking to said, "My turn to pop a flare." He came back in, and I told him I could do that next time; he answered, ok, the box is right back there."

As time rolled on, suddenly, our small compound started getting mortared. That woke everybody up. As the mortars came in, the Marines started yelling, "Get ready for an attack. After I don't know how long, small arms fire started coming in from all directions. Flares went up, and looking out the bunkers aperture for enemy targets which was hazardous to one's health, still needed to be done. Our ears were all fucked-up, but these are things one must deal with. I took out my cigarette pack, tore apart a couple of cigarettes, and used the filters as filters for earplugs; then, I offered some filters to the other Marines in the Bunker for their ears. But no attack happened, but they did not stop lobbing in mortar rounds. They are not very accurate but deadly in their explosions—light small arms fire, but no attack yet. We had great expectations of an enemy advance on our position, especially considering the Mortar attack on us.

It seemed like hours had passed, and the morning was getting brighter and brighter. Then the attack came from the north and east at a distance ground up type firing, with a lot of fire. Targets were still hard to see, but we kept their heads down, and at a distance they were, even when they did stand up a little, they were challenging targets to hit. We knew sappers would try to blow our wire had to crawl into position, but in the din of light, we now were getting, they had very little chance of that happening. Their time was slipping and fading away for them quickly. Over time the targets we were hitting were mounting up for them as they got closer and closer to us. We got word that Marines from Echo-2 were coming to us and bringing ammo and firepower. Of course, we had no way of telling how many enemies we were involved with, but someone here had glassed a large enemy force moving toward the airbase and river from our Village. We heard some very big booms north of us, a long distance away by the river and airfield, with dots of slow-moving planes that we couldn't tell if they were landing or taking off, with large plums of black smoke rising from that area.

As time passed, the assault on us got closer and closer. We figured the enemy would pour through the gate and breach more of our wire any time. It was becoming a target-rich battlefield, but we were still holding our own. Over the comm, we were told to try to hold back our ammo and pick good solid targets as much as possible. Out of six 20 round mags, I was reloading the last two. Some Marines on the Base smoked the area around the dead enemies and started recovering weapons and ammo. I was not in that group, but those brave Marines made a few trips, which re-armed us for a bit longer. I requested a Bandler of a 100 rounds for a M-

60 machine gun to the Marine on the com, and I received that banner just as my receiver locked back in place about 20 mins later with my last loaded Mag. It seemed that during this time something was pulling them off of us. Some of us thought the relief Marines were hitting them, giving us time and the break, we needed to re-arm ourselves. The timing couldn't have happened any better. Artillery was pounding the Village, and we knew help was coming.

We noticed a significant battle was taking place north and west and south of us, and the enemy that had been attacking us was moving in that direction. The incoming fire was waning that afternoon; The radio told us that all hell was going to break loose, and everyone to stay in our bunkers. The Marine air wing was coming in to pick us up. As the Rock star Little Richard would say, "Great balls of Fire." God bless them as the ground shook. When the Hilarious rocket fire abated, the choppers came in and extracted us from our death trap. As short as I am in my Nam tour, everyone at that compound was saved. As we lifted off, we could see how large of a battle it was, and we had only played a small part in it; all I can say is, "Amazing." The fight of Lo Giang rages on behind and below us, as we banked out toward the airbase in Da Nang.

Later I would make a another failed attempt to see Dennis before heading back to my Base, the battle on south Hwy 1 was too much for me to forge through farther south with the embattled area of Hwy 1 again, and it was getting dark and late. I didn't see the truck he was supposed to be on when an Army officer on Hwy 1 approached and thanked me for all my help and said, "Now Marine, leave my field of battle and go back to your parent unit." I said, "Yes sir," and saluted him, and said that I would be heading north on Hwy 1 to the Bridge and back to my Base at FLC. My plan was stopping at the Bridge and then to the airbase if I could make it to the bridge alive as the fighting was starting to wind down a little along the combat busy Hwy. 1.

Chapter 7

Stumbled And Fumbled

Returning north along Hwy 1 was precarious because the subdued light with light and dark shadows blended together. The action was starting to wane, but the rounds still flying through the air and were still lethal, further subduing my progress.

The army troops were moving back and forth along the highway. I could see the Bridge off in the distance when I noticed some movement off to my right. Vietnamese hidden in the bush; I quickly shouldered my weapon and moved closer. Upon seeing their frightened faces, three Vietnamese soldiers were frozen as I had the drop on them. I told them to stand up sternly and loudly in my broken Vietnamese. Full of newly minted combat gear, they came out by my command. With the motion of my weapon, I had them move into a more lighted area just off the road. All three were wounded in one way or another, with blood smeared around on them. Another shock to me was how young they were.

Far From the Bridge

One spoke some English and asked me if I would shoot them. I told him to drop their weapons and slowly remove his gear and then their gear, or I would shoot. He told them what I said in Vietnamese and they started to release their weapons and equipment, wincing in pain. I move them in my direction, away from their gear. I told them in English to remove their hats and shirts, which he repeated to them in Vietnamese. Then I instructed him to use the shirts to wrap their wounds which they had many. After a short time, I guided them to the road. As the activity along this road was somewhat busy, it was hard to get anyone's attention; noise and all urgency going on.

I finally got a soldier's attention not far from the Bridge. He asked me if they were south Vietnamese soldiers, and I thought for a moment. I knew they were VC or NVA, with new uniforms, gear, and the AKs we left behind down the road. I answered, "I don't know." And he went to get medical help. I also knew that the truth might lead maybe to their death. I looked at these battle-beaten boys who could not have been more than 13 to 15 years old, and the one that could speak English put his two hands together like in prayer and said, "Thank you, Marine." In my mind, I thought, wow, he knew I was a Marine. A long while had passed, and I thought they had forgotten all about us. About then, a bunch of soldiers came running over to us and said they had to take the three Vietnamese to a Medical dust-off area to be transported to the Med-Center by chopper. I looked at the boys, and one of them had passed out and limp. This soldier picked him up and ran off with him, and the other two Vietnamese boys were helped quickly in the same direction. Silently, in my mind, I wished them luck. I also knew I had done the right thing during this ongoing battle.

Crossing The Bridge

As I stumbled and fumbled down this highway north, beaten and tired, from the lack of sleep and everything else. I don't even remember crossing the Bridge. Wondering down through the Village south of the airfield, I was spent and needed to collect myself if I was going to make it back to FLC. By then, I was left with the dilemma of whether to turn left to Freedom and take the back road or continue down Hwy. 1, the long way back. I couldn't tell if this shack was a business or someone's home, but I entered it anyway. By the entrance, there was a place that looked good for resting and smoking. I took my Helmet off and relaxed. I was so exhausted I don't remember falling asleep. I must have just pasted out. Suddenly I was startled awake and found myself amid a Vietnamese family. I looked at them, and they looked at me the two young children near me, maybe five or six years old, when the boy and girl giggled. The teenage girl to my left smiled at me when the mama-son came into the room and offered me some hot tea and crackers. They asked me in surprisingly good English if I was ok, and I responded with a warm yes. They told me that this was their shop and home. They sold cookies and bread to people on the highway. It was very early in the morning, and that the fighting that was going on around them scarred them a lot. They asked me to stay with them, protect them from the VC, and showed me the bullet holes in the roof and walls.

I could see that this family had fashioned a basement into a bunker with the help of some Navy men that had built it for them almost a year ago. The top of the Bunker was their tiled floor of the first level, the shop, and the kitchen, with a sleeping room and living room in the back. It was all laid out perfectly. They complained that the tin roof leaked from the holes, and they didn't have time to fix it yet with sandbags to cover them. She also said they had little to no business since the fighting started. The young teenage girl told me her father had joined the ARVNs, and they had not heard from him for over a year. I told the girl that her father and mother had made a beautiful daughter. I saddled up and got ready to leave back to Base. I had a bunch of MPC in my pocket and gave it to the girl. The girl cried and said this was too much money for the Tea and crackers. I told her that that was not enough for their hospitality and thanked her and her family. She quickly said she was 18 and would love me to see her and her family again. I was flattered and told her that I might come back in the near future. As I neared the front door, she whispered in my ear that she had fallen in love with me. I smiled at her with a thank you, sweetheart. She announced to her family that I called her sweetheart.

I had safely made it back to my Base and went straight to see Gunny. He gave me time off after my dissertation, leading me up to today. I told him about Echo 4, but not about my venture on Hwy. 1 after Echo 4 since it was a detail that had no value to my mission. The second Lt. had yet to make it back from An-Hoa, and the Base was busy with everything going on during this TET Offensive. Since I was gone, the Base had been hit again from the Antenna valley area. The combat action was still going on in south Da Nang area and the mountains to our north. I also discovered that Saigon and Hue City were still heavily involved. I bumped into Master Sargent Borders, and he said he might need Sgt. Ski to go back to Echo 4 tomorrow.

I showered, relaxed, and waited for my next orders. With my short-timer status here in the Nam, I was getting the feeling that I should stay in the Nam. I felt like no one could do my job as I could. But then again, my survival instinct told me otherwise.

It was telling me to leave while I could. But was that really smarter? I still had over a month to go here, and the war had just gotten slightly more extensive and intense. Things could go south real quick, and maybe they'd need me here more than my desire to go home.

The confusion was making me feel more anxious,

73

But that is the life of a Marine, like an alcoholic, living life one day at a time in a war zone. You don't know what tomorrow brings until you survive it.

You don't know what you would do; you just knew you were addicted to what you did, even when you knew it was harmful and possibly life-threatening.

Echo 4

Book, Echo 4

This is my after thought

Christmas 1967 has already passed without a hitch. Most of Vietnam had few violations of the Christmas ceasefire, and the calendar of New Year, January 1st, has passed midnight with little breaking news fire fights across the country. Intel had warned our Command that something big was in the works, but nobody knew when or where it would start or occur. The Intel was so strong that MACV had the bases throughout Vietnam try to trigger it prematurely with carefully orchestrated fake Base hits, fake Firefights, and responding troops hiding in the field. Putting the entire country on full alert from a stand-down position. But nothing happened during the first week of January 1968. This started the thinking that it may happen during the Lunar Chinese New Year of TET. During this time, every year, the South Vietnam Government would send the ARVN troops home for a holiday with rotating leave. We would be ordered to stand down and try not to interfere with this celebration. Never a conflict. Even the VC would take a break and mix with the population unarmed while the NVA stood down and in place. But this was different, and we felt it was different

Since before Christmas, the Army had been moving Divisions north along highway 1, which kind of hugs the coast with mountain passes to cross along the way. It was a huge movement, and logistical support was spread out all along the highway with replenishment way points. Some elements moved faster than others, but no ambushes were reported. At the same time, the Marines in Khe Shan were fully engaged with the NVA on both hills 881 and Hill 861, and Khe Shan dominated the News with President Johnson saying, "This will not be another, Bien, Bien, Phu."

This story begins shortly after the 1968 TET Offensive begins, with some small Marine Outposts just south of the Da Nang airbase at the Cau Do River; a Marine Outpost called Echo 4 was just 2 km south of the river near the village of Lo Giang, which was a very kickback Outpost with no combat experience even this late in the TET Offensive. Little did these 11 Marines and a few Vietnamese PFs (Popular Forces) know that the Army's 1st Battalion 6th Infantry, 198th Light Infantry Brigade, Americal Division moved in north and west of Echo 4 position from Chu Lai. Soon, the Marines of Echo 4 would be fighting for their existence, and the elements of the 1st Battalion 6th Infantry would be fighting for theirs. The story will piece together a battle that, for historical purposes, would only be second to the infamous battle for Hamburger Hill, which suffered 39 KIAs in 10 days. Where 1st Bn 6th Inf had suffered in 10 hours, 34 KIA's for a battalion-sized unit is a tragedy. All Marines in ECHO 4 would survive, but the ECHO 2 Marine relief force lost 12 KIA, three captured, one wounded, and only one escaped.

This is their story; this is their battle and observed and participated in by eyewitnesses mentioned and not mentioned so that the story can be told, and their sacrifice can be told. This battle never made headlines, never was brought forward in this form, until now. After four days of fighting, Americal Division units killed 308 enemies, while the Marines accounted for 411 enemies KIA. There was a total of 31 crew-served weapons captured. The fierce fighting concluded with Valorous metals for those who survived and did not survive the experience. The display of extraordinary heroism and devotion to duty. In keeping with the highest traditions of military service. This is that War story for everyone to know, with detail of both Marines and Army personnel. I know because I was there, stuck between a rock and a hard spot, looking at Sgt. Dennis Hammond. I was short, and so was he, both of us are from Michigan. My name is Bob Le Beau, L/Cpl. RC Lebeau, USMC, stuck at Echo 4 was not of my plan. Thank you, "Tiny," for telling your story, Marine Mike Readinger, RTO, and Truck driver. But I do have photos to share. Echo 4 was my Ft. Apache. Thank God for the Army that Day on the 8th of Feb. 68. We traded our weapons for AK-47s for our final flight. At about 16:00 that afternoon, we were back at the Da Nang airbase.

I foolishly went back to Hwy. 1 to look for Dennis at the embattled site of **CAP Echo 4** to no avail, and it was getting late. **And, yes after my Marine Corps honorable discharge I went to the Philippines and visited my sweetheart. She said that her and her family were in the process of going to America.**

Photograph, from the camera of, Marine, RC LeBeau
Feb. 11th or 12th, 1968 road to Echo 4

Our return to Echo 4 after the Battle had come to a logical conclusion a couple of days later, after the 8th of Feb., sweeping for mines on our way back into the Echo 4 outpost area at Lo Giang, enemy activity was still a possibility, with a PF passing by on a bicycle in the photo above.

Appendix

Marine and Army References

and AARs of the Battle

Submitted by: Mike "Tiny" Readinger
Foxtrot 2/Echo 2 and Echo CACO

The following first-person account of the siege of Echo 4, and the subsequent loss of the reaction force sent to their aid, was provided by Mike "Tiny" Readinger. Mike, at the time, was the radioman for CAG HQs, having previously spent ten months with CAP Echo 2.

All this story has been written from memory, and Mike readily admits to the potential for erroneous information.

I hope to explain to the best of my memory and ability the history of the ECHO CAPs from early 1967 to February. I may very well miss the exact chronological order of events, but I'll do my best.

Mike "Tiny" Readinger

Echo 4

R.C. Le Beau

Although I do not remember the exact number of Echo units or the exact number of each unit by location, I do know Echo 2 and Echo 4 are correct. Echo 2 is where I served up to the right before TET, 1968 when I was called into Hoa Vang as a radioman and truck driver. Not realizing it then, this move was to eventually save my life, but it left me with many haunting memories.

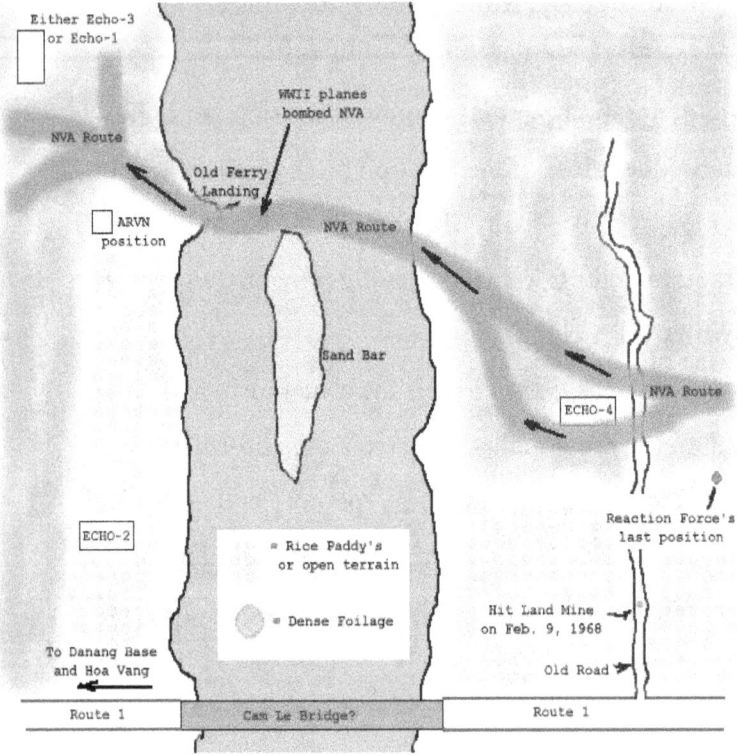

I believe there were 6 Echo units. They have strung out approx. 2-4 miles outside the perimeter of Danang Airbase. Echo-2 and Echo-4 to the south; Echo-1 to the west (close to Monkey Mountain); Echo-3 to the east, and Echo-4 & 5 to the north. Of course, to CAP'ers, being this close to Da Nang was considered gravy duty, which for the most part it was.....until February 8, 1968.

One would think that being this close to Da Nang, one would have the best air and fire support in the country. This was not to be the case, as we shall see. For some silly reason, the only way we could get support from Da Nang was through the MP battalion; no direct contacts were allowed.

On the morning of February 8th, 1968, we monitored radio traffic between a "bird-dog" and Da Nang/MP battalion. This is the context of the radio log, as I remember it. *(Not remembering the call signs, I shall use "Da Nang" and "Bird-Dog")*

Bird-dog: *"Da Nang, I've got approximately 400-600 unknowns on the ground, at approximately (gave cords) 15 miles south of your position!"*

Da Nang: *"We have some units working in that area, but nothing close to that size. Can you identify?"*

Bird-dog: *"Negative, Da Nang...they have moved under the canopy..."*

Da Nang: *"Advise, stay on station for as long as possible, and we will work it on this end."*

(End of this log....no other transmissions were ever heard.)

Author's Notes

What no one knew at this time was that the NVA and some locals had massed for an attack on Da Nang on the 7th, hopefully under cover of darkness, but due to delays, they did not get into position until after daylight on the 8th. At this point, we believe their strategy was to wait until the darkness of the evening of the 8th. However, after being spotted by the Bird-dog, their plans changed rapidly.

(Please See Map)

Under concealment of the dense foliage, they made their way to the perimeter of ECHO-4, realizing that we probably wouldn't fire on our own unit as long as they didn't over-run it. Once again, they hoped they could hold this position until nightfall. At this point, ECHO-4 came under intense fire, and 11 Marines and a handful of PFs held off the hordes for several hours.

No Marines or PFs at Echo-4 were lost, although a few received serious wounds.

Now this part, for some reason, I cannot pinpoint exactly when it happened. Perhaps later events have taken their toll on my memory. I only know that it happened prior to the loss of the reaction force because Sgt. Ramos was on that reaction force.

At some point of time on the 8th, prior to the loss of the reaction force, Sgt Ramos and I drove from Hoa Vang to Echo-2. We had just arrived when 200-300 NVA made the river crossing towards Da Nang (Please See Map). I remember trying to get the MP battalion to react to the situation, but I could not get them to understand our location. They seemed to not be able to comprehend the fact that the enemy was that close and was more interested in my radio procedure than the help that I was trying to obtain. For whatever reason, no help was obtained from the MP battalion.

To this day, I have no idea why or how, but two small WWII aircraft piloted by South Vietnamese arrived and made immediate hits on the NVA crossing the river (Please See Map). My only opinion is that our Vietnamese troops at Hoa Vang were monitoring our radio, heard how far our MP battalion had their head up their ass and made a call for their own air support. But for whatever reason, it probably saved Echo-3 as the surviving NVA could do nothing but disperse as rapidly as possible once in the area of Echo-3 (or Echo-1).

For the record, I believe this is where the "288" NVA (as previously quoted) were killed. Certainly, 288 is a very inflated number. Perhaps 100-150, but certainly not 288. The sad part is many of these were South Vietnamese that the

NVA forced across the river as cover. Unfortunately, 500-pound bombs and 20mm shells couldn't tell the difference.

My last comment on this event is as follows. It is not intended to degrade the ARVNs but to place credit where credit is due. (Please See Map)

Approximately a month prior to the river crossing, the ARVNs set up an 8-10-man position, as shown on the map. Every day they would practice firing their 50mm. When the fatal day came, we watched them boogie...except for one lonely Chu-Hoi, who we found later lying beside the .50mm which he had destroyed...probably as his last action.

At some point in the early afternoon on the 8th, Echo-4 transmitted a request for ammo, stating they were on their last radio battery. Now, probably due to the fact that most of Vietnam were being hit at the same moment, there were no aircraft available at Da Nang for re-supply. Even if there had been, between the small size of ECHO-4's compound, and the heavy weapons of the enemy in the area, it would have made this feat almost impossible.

Due to the critical nature of ECHO-4's plight, a call went out to Echos 1, 2, and 3 for volunteers to form a reaction force to re-supply and reinforce ECHO-4's position. At this time, no one had any idea of the size of the enemy force. A truck was dispatched to bring the volunteers to Hoa Vang.

Now...here's where the tough part begins.

When the truck pulled up in front of my radio hooch, the first person that I noticed was Dennis Hammond, my best and closest friend. We had served almost ten months together at Echo-2, both loving to hunt and fish.... we were naturals. Dennis had two tours, saving all his money for a Corvette and some land in Canada. He and his brother were going to start a hunting and fishing camp there. At the time, Dennis had less than three weeks left in his tour and an immediate discharge upon arriving home. Here is the conversation that took place:

Me: *"Ham-bone, what in the fuck are you doing! Your too fucking short for this kinda shit!"*

Dennis: *"Hey buds, I been here for two fucking years and can't see where I've accomplished shit. This will be my last chance!"*

And it was.

The truck pulled away as I acknowledged several other members of Echos 1, 2, and 3. I was denied going by my C.O., as I was to be the only source of radio contact.

The truck proceeded just south of Cam Le bridge (Please See Map), to where the reaction force started their assault. They proceeded east across the open terrain for approximately 500 yards. Then they came to a deep irrigation ditch which they used for cover until they were within a few yards of the canopy that surrounded ECHO 4.

At this point, the fifteen-man reaction force walked head long into a 200-300-man ambush.

Here is the radio log, as I remember it. It's pretty accurate. It should be. I get to hear it almost every night. Only the part where the first contact was made is included.

I'd also like to note the calmness of Capt. Joselane's voice, right to the end. He was a fine Marine Officer.

Capt. Joselane = Echo Actual. Myself = Echo Mama.

Actual: *"Mama, we've just started taking heavy fire. I'll give you some numbers in a minute."*

(30-40 seconds later)

Actual: *"Mama, we're getting chewed up. See if you can get Echo 4 to come in from the north and help."*

(A few seconds later)

Actual: *"We aren't gonna get out...there are too many...they're all over us....no way out. Don't send anyone else in here................tell my wife I love her........."*

(End of log)

Author's Note: Echo 4 could not have helped; they were still under siege.

From beginning to end, this action could not have lasted more than 3 minutes.

My memory also fails me here. I can't remember exactly when they did an "Air-Extract" of Echo-4, but it was accomplished.

The evening of February 8th:

Due to failing light, an exact location of the reaction force, shortage of manpower, etc., 2nd CAG made the call that we would re-group and wait for the morning of the 9th. This was not a very popular choice with the remaining folks at Hoa Vang, and it almost prompted a mutiny. A tank company, I don't remember which, was contacted for support since we knew we couldn't get anything out of the MP battalion. We had perhaps 10-12 troops assembled at Hoa Vang when the tank's C.O. informed us that his equipment was too heavy for the Cam Le bridge.

At that point, it was aborted, and we were forced to wait until the morning of the 9th.

It seems as if this night lasted for weeks. For one Marine lying wounded, I'm sure it lasted for eternity.

I don't remember his first name as he was a newbie at either Echo-1 or Echo-3, but "Greeno" may have been the luckiest man in the world on that night. In trying to keep a chronological order to the events, I will tell his story in a moment.

Morning of the 9th:

At first light, another reaction force was assembled at Hoa Vang. We proceeded south of the Cam Le bridge and departed the truck there (junction of Highway 1 and old road

[Please See Map]). From there, we walked toward the area where we believed the reaction force would be found. In the following description of what we found, I only include for the sake of the heroism that had left a painted picture.

As we walked east across the open terrain, we came upon a very deep irrigation ditch which we immediately used for cover, not realizing at that time that the reaction force had done the same thing. As we moved farther east, we began seeing pieces of shrapnel and other signs of an intense battle. Our Aussie point then came upon the first casualty.

I'm not going to go into any great detail here. I will only comment on certain things for historical purposes.

Greeno was where he had laid all night with seven wounds. He had applied his own tourniquets. He told this story, which he told me again a few days later in a hospital in Japan.

Greeno: *"They let us get right to the tree line before they hit us. We thought because of the ditch, we had an excellent cover, but that wasn't true. There were so many of them; they had good coverage of that part of the ditch and just kept blooping rocket grenades."*

"They captured Hammond, Zawtocki, and Talbot. We saw them being led away."

"We tried to attack into the ambush, but it was too late. They had too good a position just inside the tree line. And there were too many."

"Gifford was a hero. Every time I saw him, he was moving to a new position to treat someone else. He moved as if the heavy fire was the least of his concerns."

Author's Note: When we found Greg "bac-si" Gifford, we observed the following:

He had used almost all of his medical pack. We found several Marines that he had treated. Although showing multiple wounds, he had not treated himself. He was found at the side of Pete Cruz with his last roll of gauze still clutched in his hand. An empty clip for his .45 was found beneath him. The rest he had tried to bury beside him, probably not noticeable by the NVA in the darkness that soon followed.

Greg performed far beyond the highest tradition of the Combat Corpsman. His dignified manners when at Echo-2 were way beyond his young years. If anyone ever deserved the Congressional Medal of Honor, he did. He and his family were cheated.

Continuing with Greeno:

Greeno: *"I was eventually knocked out. When I came to, it was dark, and the NVA were walking all over the area. Anytime they came close to me, I played dead. They searched and kicked me several times that night. At one point early this morning, I thought they had left. I raised my head to look. There was a lone NVA radioman not more than ten feet away, looking directly at me. He motioned with his hand for me to lay back down.*

I'll never forget that. Soon after that, he and the others left the area."

Go To:

NVA Radioman: Why He Let Greeno Live

That afternoon, while trying to get a truck into the area to evacuate the KIA, I found a land mine with a deuce-and a half. I spent some time at a hospital in Japan. Then, for some unexplainable reason, I chose to go back for my last 30 days. I spent those 30 days at Hoa Vang, with almost daily visits to the Echo. But it was never to be the same. The only happy reminders were our local South Vietnamese villagers, who never forgot our friendship or sacrifices.

Ti, I pray that you made it.

CAP Echo 4 Story Update

On May 12, 2002, I received an e-mail from Wayne Johnson, the historian for the Army's 1st Battalion 6th Infantry. Wayne had read Mike Readinger's story about the Echo 4 attack, and he wanted the opportunity to communicate with Mike to complete his history from the perspective of the CAP Marines involved. Wayne's account of the battle from Army records, with Mike Readinger's assistance, is at:

• Task Force Miracle

The Reaction Force:

Here is a list of the reaction force KIA. There were three survivors listed below

- Sgt. Palmer, who somehow managed to walk out of the ambush.

- Don Talbot was captured with Hammond and Zawtocki but managed to escape in the following days.

- Greeno (see story above).

I can account for all except Dennis Hammond, whose remains are yet to be returned. After many, many years of research, I shall make this statement:

Although search teams have, on several occasions, been to the approximate site and have failed, evidently, no one is willing to filter through the facts that are available. Government documents alone have the area of burial location pinpointed down to less than 1/8 of an acre.

Robert Garwood's book, for whatever he was or wasn't, provides excellent information. Garwood could probably walk right to the spot. The credibility of his facts about Hammond is also substantiated by the book "Seven Survivors," a book co-authored by the survivors of the same POW camp where Hammond died.

The last information that I have is because of the rough terrain and/or weather conditions, lack of access, and lack of manpower and heavy equipment, and they are at almost a standstill. To that, I shall make this final comment.

To whom it may concern: USMC? US Government? Bill Clinton?

It sure seems ironic that when we have a need to send men and women into combat anywhere in the world, there is never a shortage of manpower, heavy equipment, or a will to commit. How much effort would it take to find one lost soul in 1/8 of an acre? Please don't reference me to the search teams. That's where I got the information about the manpower and equipment shortage.

Time is growing short, and I find each day that "Semper Fi" may very well be intended as a one-way street. I was a Marine, I will always be a Marine, and I will continue to count on the USMC to lead the way in bringing Dennis home......soon. How can we continue the tradition if we don't?

Here is the list of the reaction force KIAs. I have pictures of several from previous occasions that I will publish soon.

- Last Name: Basso

First Name: Michele

ID. NO: 2104289

Service: USMC

Rank: Sgt.

Grade: E5

MOS: 0311

Age: 21

Home: North   White   Plains

State: N.Y.

Casualty   Date: 1968-02-08

Birthdate: 1946-10-15

Religion: Roman   Catholic

Marital   Status: Single

Panel: 38E

Line: 020

- Last   Name: Cruz

First   Name: Peter   Frank

IDNO: 2328004

Service: USMC

Rank: Cpl.

Grade: E4

MOS: 0353

Age: 21

Home: Chualar

State: CA

Casualty   Date: 1968-02-08

Birthdate: 1946-09-21

Marital   Status: Single

Panel: 38E

Line: 024

- Last Name: Jackson
First Name: Johnnie Bruce
ID NO: 2307345
Service: USMC
Rank: LCpl
Grade: E3
MOS: 3531
Age: 20
Home: Fort Worth
State: TX
Casualty Date: 1968-02-08
Birthdate: 1947-08-14
Marital Status: Married
Panel: 38E
Line: 030

- Last Name: Joselane
First Name: Howard Leo
ID NO: 080626
Service: USMC
Rank: Cpt.
Grade: O-3
MOS: 0302
Age: 29
Home: Chicago

State: IL

Casualty Date: 1968-02-08

Birthdate: 1938-02-18

Marital Status: Married

Panel: 38E

Line: 031

- Last Name: Kinney

First Name: Lee Charles

IDNO: 2259949

Service: USMC

Rank: Cpl.

Grade: E4

MOS: 3041

Age: 21

Home: Welch

State: MN

Casualty Date: 1968-02-08

Birthdate: 1947-01-09

Marital Status: Single Panel: 38E

Line: 031

- Last Name: Lamorte

First Name: Arthur William

IDNO: 2332430

Service: USMC

Rank: LCpl.

Grade: E3

MOS: 3516

Age: 19

Home: Baltimore

State: MD

Casualty Date: 1968-02-08

Birthdate: 1948-04-06

Marital Status: Single

Panel: 38E

Line: 031

- Last Name: Metcalf

First Name: Jimmy Allen

IDNO: 2329760

Service: USMC

Rank: LCpl.

Grade: E3

MOS: 0811

Age: 21

Home: Dallas

State: TX

Casualty Date: 1968-02-08

Birthdate: 1946-03-28

Marital Status: Single

Panel: 38E

Line: 033

- Last   Name: Murphy

First   Name: John   Robert

IDNO: 2320111

Service: USMC

Rank: LCpl.

Grade: E3

MOS: 1341

Age: 19

Home: Yorktown   Heights

State: NY

Casualty   Date: 1968-02-08

Birthdate: 1948-11-08

Marital   Status: Single

Panel: 38E

Line: 034

- Last   Name: Ramos

First   Name: Frank   Jr.

IDNO: 1302158

Service: USMC

Rank: SSgt.

Grade: E6

MOS: 0369

Age: 33

Home: Youngstown

State: OH

Casualty Date: 1968-02-08

Birthdate: 1934-08-25

Marital Status: Single

Panel: 38E

Line: 037

- Last Name: Sirianni

First Name: Daniel Edward

IDNO: 2289227

Service: USMC

Rank: LCpl

Grade: E3

MOS: 2143

Age: 20

Home: Buffalo

State: NY

Casualty Date: 1968-02-08

Birthdate: 1948-01-08

Marital Status: Single

Panel: 38E

Line: 039

- Last Name: Hammond

First Nave: Dennis Wayne

IDNO: 375506720

Service: USMC

Rank: Sgt.

Grade: E5

MOS: 3111

Age: 23

Home: Detroit

State: MI

Casualty Date: 1970-03-07

Birthdate: 1946-04-26

Marital Status: Single

Panel: 38E

Line: 029

- Last Name: Zawtocki

First Name: Joseph Stanley, Jr.

IDNO: 115362341

Service: USMC

Rank: Sgt.

Grade: E5

MOS: 2511

Age: 39

Home: Utica

State: NY

Casualty Date: 1969-12-24

Birthdate: 1946-05-16

Marital Status: Single

Panel: 38E

Line: 042

Corpsman:

- Last Name: Gifford

First Name: Gregory Allen

IDNO: 6963920

Service: USN

Rank: HM3

Grade: E4

MOS: HM3

Age: 19

Home: Billings

State: MT

Casualty Date: 1968-02-08

Birthdate: 1948-03-11

Marital Status: Single

Panel: 38E

Line: 028

- Last Name: Johnson

First Name: Charles Eugene

IDNO: 5960991

Service:		USN
Rank:		HN
Grade:		E3
MOS:		HN
Age:		23
Home:		Toledo
State:		OR
Casualty	Date:	1968-02-08
Birthdate:		1944-10-21
Marital	Status:	Single
Panel:		38E
Line: 030		

A Shadow on the Wall

It was 2:00 a.m. in the morning when he came upon the   wall...
A dark black "V" of granite, it stands not very tall.

The timing was premeditated, and he had to be alone...
For it's very hard to hear a voice that's etched in stone.

He paced those wings of black, looking for a friend...
And to reflect upon a moment in time, to a place where they'd once been.

The panel suddenly appeared, and the voice was once again   heard...

A long-lost friend had been found among the whisper of his word.

In the silence of the night, it echoed from the wall... *"You can let it go now, and thanks for coming to call."*

And then he moved away, and the silhouetted wall began to fade... But looking back, he noticed......his shadow....*it had stayed......for those who cannot...*

C.M. Readinger / "Twist" / "Tiny" III MAF, 2nd CAG Echo-2 and Hoa Vang

NVA

Radioman

Submitted by: Mike Readinger Echo 2 & 2nd. CAG HQ

Editor's Note: I have read Al Hemingway's book, and I read Mike Readinger's story as I posted it to the Web Site. However, I did not make the connection between Hemingway & Readinger as it relates to "Greeno" and the NVA Radioman.

Our thanks to James Larsen for making the connection.

The NVA Radioman

From The Echo 4 Story: *"...the NVA radioman motioned me to lay back down.... I'll never forget that"*

Tim,

I've been hanging on to this for a couple of weeks now, mainly out of shock and disbelief that I stumbled across it thanks to James "Vini" Larsen and, of course, you and the CAP Web Site.

Let me explain...

I got an e-mail from James Larsen over a year ago. At that time, he explained that he had visited the VVHP and had seen my writings on Dennis Hammond. As he had happened to have worn (and still wears) Dennis' POW bracelet, he was interested in finding out all he could talk about Dennis.

We communicated several times over the next few months, and I gave him the names of the two books that he could read about Dennis while he was a POW.

Then, when I found your CAP site, had my pictures scanned and wrote the ECHO-4 story, I invited him there. From that day on, he seemed to be totally dedicated to researching everything he could find out about Dennis. All of this led to his mail, which I am forwarding to you.

As you remember, in the E-4 story, Greeno had played dead, and his life was saved by an NVA radioman......I never until now had any idea, or did anyone else that I was able to talk to, why the NVA radioman did what he did. As you will see in the forwarded message...we do now!!!!

Forwarded   Message   Follows

Date: Sun,   08   Jun   1997   12:14:00   -0800

From: James   A   Larsen

Organization: Tektronix,   Inc.

To: Mike   Readinger

Subject: Greeno

Check   it   out

Our War Was Different, by Al Hemingway, Pgs. 85-88

An   account   is   given   by   B.   Keith   Cossey

2nd   CAG,   1966-1968

Quote (just before 1968 TET)

During my friend's visit, we noticed a kid crouched under a tree, very skinny and looking exhausted. He was too young to be potentially harmful, maybe 11 or 12, so we invited him inside our fortified compound to have some food and a sheltered place to sleep before moving on. Marines were always suckers for orphans......

...17 out of the 19 volunteers were killed. Only 2 survived: Corp. Talbot and my friend. My friend, wounded by shrapnel, was on the ground trying to help another CAP friend of ours who was choking to death after having been shot in the throat. An NVA soldier came from behind and bayoneted them both. When he regained consciousness, my friend saw that he was the only American left alive. The NVA was torturing to death the SV PFs. An NVA soldier spotted my friend moving and motioned to the others he'd go over and kill him. But then an NVA radioman ran over and intercepted the other soldier, gesturing that he'd do the job for him. The fully helmeted and uniformed radio operator came and stood over my friend. It was the kid we'd befriended a week or two previously. The kid motioned for him to lay his head down and pointed his rifle at him. At least, my friend thought, he was going to make it short and sweet and was not going to screw with me like his buddies are with the PFS. The kid then fired next to his head purposely and strode off to report that he had accomplished his mission. That act of kindness we had performed earlier had saved my friend's life......

Tet '68: Task Force Miracle-- the Battle for Lo Giang and CAP Echo 4

Background Information.

In January 1968, the U.S. Military Assistance Command, Vietnam (USMACV) totaled Nearly 500,000 and had taken over much of the large-scale unit warfare from the South Vietnamese. III MAF controlled allied military forces in the I Corps area of northern South Vietnam. The US 1st Marine Division and 51st ARVN Regiment provided protection for The Da Nang area. Enemy forces in the northern I Corps area were controlled directly by the North Vietnamese.

III MAF, the US Marine command in I Corps, emphasized the small unit war in the villages. Consequently, they developed the Combined Action Program (CAP) that assigned a squad Of US Marines to a village Vietnamese Popular Forces platoon. One of these units, CAP Echo 4 was located in the village of Lo Giang (1), several miles south of Da Nang. The objective of these and similar units was to create a bond with the local village The population that would sever their relationship with the guerrillas and VC infrastructure. While the Marines emphasized these small unit relations, the MACV forces were directed At defeating the enemy's main forces. The battle for Lo Giang was conducted by the US Army soldiers from the 1st Battalion 6th Infantry and the attempted relief and eventual extraction of the Marines at CAP Echo, 4 demonstrated the relationship between these two very Different approaches to the war.

The 1968 TET Offensive begins.

On 27 Jan 68, the Communists announced their seven-day cease fire for Tet 1968. Several

Days later, however, they launched the largest offensive of the war. Attacks began in the Da Nang area on 30 Jan 68. At 0230, sappers attacked the III MAF compound in Da Nang. About one hour later, enemy forces attacked the I Corps headquarters complex in Hoa Vang.

The following extract from the official US Marine Corps history shows the following:

"Under cover of darkness, elements of the VC R-20th and V-25th Battalions had crossed the Cau Do River. With covering fire provided by 81mm and 82mm mortars, about a reinforced The company reached the I Corps headquarters compound actually located within the city of Da Nang just outside the northern perimeter of the main air base. The fighting within the compound Continued until daylight. After their breaching of the outer defenses, the enemy squad fired B-40 Rockets at the headquarters building but then fought a delaying action, waiting for reinforcements. These reinforcements never came. The bulk of the enemy attack force remained in Hoa Vang Village bogged down in a firefight with local PF and Regional Force troops reinforced by a Combined Action platoon, E-3."

"At Da Nang, on the 30th, the fighting did not subside with the coming of daylight. Elements of The VC R-20th and local force units that participated in the attack on Hoa Vang and I Corps Headquarters attempted to escape the dragnet of Marine and ARVN forces. While the 1st MP The battalion, supported by the 1st Tank Battalion, established blocking positions north of the Cau Do River, the ARVN 3d Battalion, 51st Regiment, swept the sector south of the river. Caught east of the Cam La Bridge and Route 1, on a small island formed by the convergence of the Cau Do, a small tributary of the river, and the Vien Dien River, the VC turned to fight. A Combined Action platoon at 0830 saw a number of VC attempting to swim across the Cau Do to the island."

In the fighting that followed, the 3rd Battalion, 5th Marines, and ARVN forces managed to kill 102 NVA and VC by use of artillery and tactical air strikes in the vicinity of Lo Giang (2) on 30 Jan 68. Many of the enemies were killed as they attempted to cross the Cau Do River.

[Details about the attacks of Da Nang and Hoa Vang are found at this *link*.]

[Looking south at the ferry crossing via BT 033733 on the Cau Do River east of Hoa Vang,
Approximately 2 km. Southeast of the Da Nang airfield. This 1968 photo was taken by Mike "Tiny" Readinger (CAP Echo 2 and HQ) several months before the TET offensive and is almost
A shot of the exact path taken by the NVA. The village of Lo Giang and CAP Echo 4 were located about 2 km south of the river.]

On 31 Jan 68, Communist forces launched major attacks in 39 province capitals throughout The country, and in Saigon and Hue. On the night of 2-3, Feb 68, 28 122mm rockets fell on Da Nang. Elsewhere in I Corps, ground attacks on the Marine garrison at Khe Sanh Began on 5 Feb 68. On 7 Feb 68, the daring and successful attack by NVA forces at the Lang Vei Special Forces camp west of Khe Sanh captured worldwide media attention. That attack featured the use of NVA PT 76 light armored tanks. The Marines at Khe Sanh Refused to come to the aid of US Special Forces soldiers who were being overrun by the Enemy armor.

On 7 Feb 68, the MACV commander, General Westmoreland, called for a meeting with The III MAF commander, General Cushman. Concerned that III MAF had not reacted Properly to the Lang Vei episode and that inadequate precautions had been taken to Defend Da Nang, and General Westmoreland ordered the Americal Division to supply several Infantry battalions to bolster the defenses south of Da Nang. III MAF planners decided to Utilize a two-battalion Army task force in the northern sector of the 3rd Battalion, 5th Marines Near highway QL1 just south of the Cau Do River. Task Force Miracle, as the force came to be named, was formed by the 1st Bn 6th Inf (198th Lt Inf Bde) and 2nd Bn 1st Inf (196th Lt Inf Brgde) from the Americal Division.]

The 1st Battalion 6th Infantry, 198th Light Infantry Brigade, Americal Division moves north.

At 1515 hours on 7 Feb 68, the 1st Bn 6th Inf was ordered to provide two Infantry companies and a command element as soon as possible to III MAF in Da Nang. Alpha Company, 1st Bn, 6th Inf (A/1-6) previously had been designated as the "sixty minute Alert company," tasked with reinforcing units elsewhere in Vietnam. By 1630 hours, they were at LZ Gator south of Chu Lai and ready to move to Da Nang. In 1735 the 131 men of Alpha company, under the command of CPT Francis X. Brennan, arrived at LZ 410, located at AT 991678. They were greeted by the commander of the marine unit at that location who was under the operational control of the 1st Marine Division. The move had happened so rapidly that" their presence left [the commander and staff of LZ 410] at a loss." Only Sketchy information about the enemy activity was available. The 1st Bn 6th Inf commander, LTC William J. Baxley Jr. evaluated the situation and ordered his two-available infantry companies to move into locations just south of the Cau Do River.

A/1-6 received their orders and moved out at 2200 hours. By 080155 Feb 68, they had arrived at Their night defensive position (NDP) BT 022714 is approximately 400 m. east of the *Cam Le Bridge.*

The 128 men of Co. C. 1st Bn 6th Inf (C/1-6) under CPT Max D. Bradley were only a few hours behind and closed on their NDP at BT 005694 by 080215 Feb 68. The plan was for both companies to move from their NDPs to the small bridge at BT 025719 and then conduct the search. And destroy missions on the island formed by the Cau Do, a tributary of the river, and the Vien Dien River with the center of mass for the operations at BT 035725.

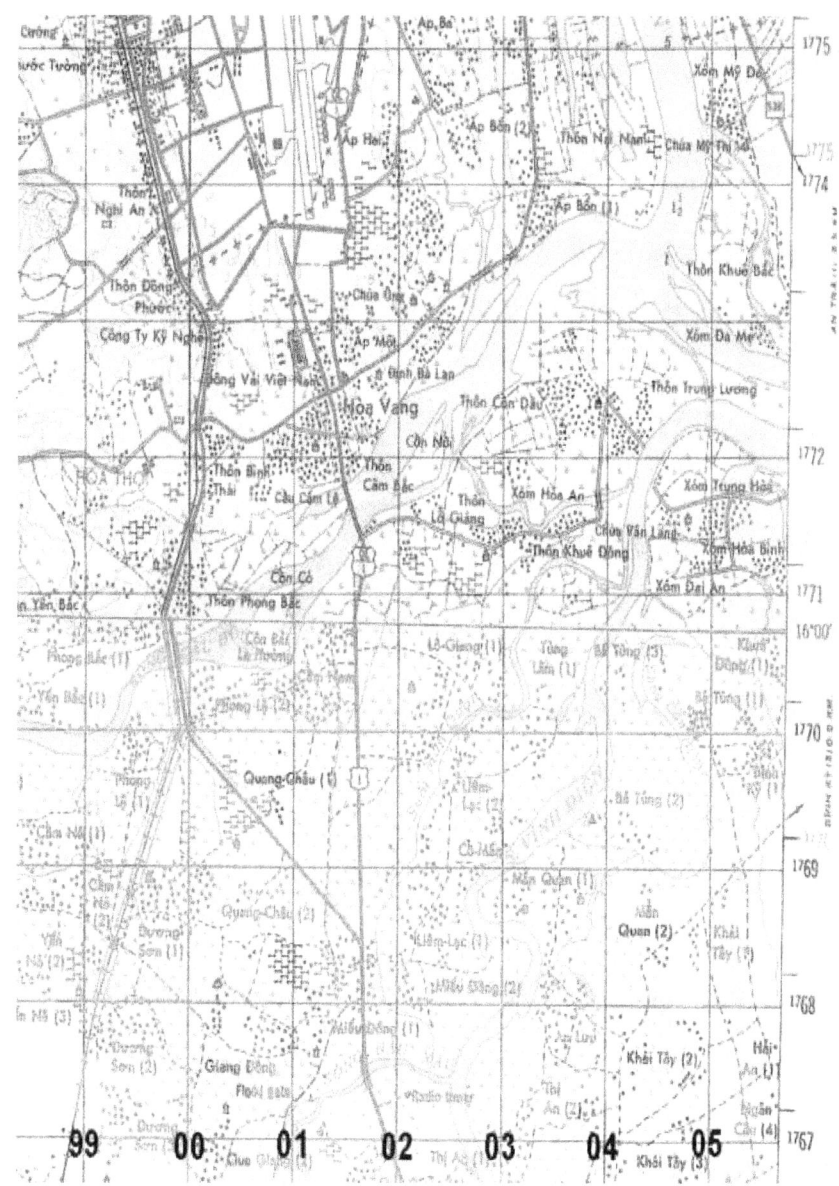

Extract of map from the US Army After Action Report
provided by Tom Hall (1/6 Inf 1967-68)
Map sheets 6641-3 (Da Nang) and 6640-4 (Dai Loc) meet

between the 70 and 71 gird lines.

View of the Da Nang airfield and base complex looking northward across the Cau Do River. Highway QL1 is visible as it approaches the Cam Le Bridge at the left of the photo. The island in the Cau Do River near the center of the photo provided a fording site for the VC during their attack on 30 Jan 68. The tree line just visible along the extreme bottom edge of the photo directly below the Cam Le Bridge concealed more than 1,000 NVA troops that were only 3,000m from the end of the airfield at Da Nang. On 8 Feb 68, the soldiers from A/1-6 Inf moved southward across the rice paddy area toward the enemy concealed in the tree line. This photo, taken from about 4,000 ft almost directly above Lo Giang, was provided by Mike Readinger

The Battle for Lo Giang and CAP Echo 4.

Enemy activity began anew early the morning of 8 Feb 68. At 0345 hours, enemy mortar rounds fell into the CAP Echo 4 compound Vic BT 028704 near Lo Giang. By daylight, enemy ground forces surrounded the CAP hamlet. At 0602 hours, the fourteen men at the location under the command of SGT B. Keith Cossey received heavy small arms fire from BT 027699. Four NVAs killed in action were found to be armed with CS grenades. All friendly units in the area were alerted of the enemy gas attack capabilities. The defenders at CAP Echo 4 had expended most of their ammunition but rearmed themselves with enemy weapons and ammunition.

As daylight arrived over the area, an OV-1 "bird dog" aircraft detected approximately 400 persons on the ground in the vicinity of Lo Giang. The aerial observer could not determine whether the soldiers were enemy or friendly before they disappeared under the canopy of trees in the area. Such brazen daylight moves by large enemy forces were a rarity. The information about a large number of suspected enemy soldiers was not communicated to the 1st

Bn   6th

Inf soldiers in the vicinity of Lo Giang.

At first light, the local "coke kids" found the soldiers of C/1-6 near BT 005 694 and began trying to sell soft drinks. One of them not only recognized the 198th Inf Bd shoulder patch but said, "198th, you come fast." In view of the attack on the Marines at CAP Echo 4, C/1-6 was ordered to move from its NDP location and to advance to the northeast toward the Lo Giang village at BT 025705.

Because of the size of the attack against CAP Echo 4, Marines from adjacent CAP units and the CAP headquarters north of the Cao Do form a reaction force under CPT Howard L. Joselane to come to their aid. One of the Marine volunteers in the force, SGT Dennis W. Hammond, had less than three weeks to go before returning to the States but stated that this was his "last chance" to accomplish something. The relief force was taken by truck across the Cam Le Bridge and south on QL1 to the Vic BT 016698, where they started toward Echo 4.

At 0826 hours, A/1-6 received a small arms fire from BT 026705. They also observed large numbers of civilians fleeing to the northeast from Lo Giang village. Having received the proper clearance, they began firing 81mm mortar rounds into the outskirts of the village. As C/1-6 began to cross highway QL1 near BT 016698 at 0940 hours, automatic weapons from enemy soldiers located in the pagoda at BT 022724 passed over their heads and increased as they advanced. The enemy fire, however, may have been directed at the Marine relief force, which was much closer to the village.

As the CAP relief force under CPT Joselane that had been attempting to reinforce CAP Echo 4 approached the tree line on the west end of Lo Giang, they suddenly came under intense fire at close range. They sought shelter in a drainage ditch just outside the tree line. Shortly after the attack began, they were overwhelmed by large numbers of VC and NVA. They radioed for help and then, a short time later, announced that they were being overrun. Capt. Joselane's last words over the radio were, *"they're all over us....no way out. Don't send anyone else in here...tell my wife I love her."* Thirteen marines in the relief force were killed by the enemy. Some of the Marines were bayoneted as they lay wounded.

Three Marines, including SGT Hammond, were captured by the NVA as POWs, but one later managed to escape. [SGT Hammond later died in captivity.] One Marine, although badly wounded, miraculously survived due to the magnanimity of an NVA radio operator who spared his life. The Marine had befriended the NVA soldier earlier while on a CAP mission. The NVA soldier had pretended to be a Vietnamese peasant who needed food and medical   attention.

.

[Note: The harrowing nature of the ordeal suffered by the Marines in the relief force and their incredible bravery has been spelled out in detail in an excellent story prepared by Mike "Tiny" Readinger that can be found on the Marine *CAP web site*. Those few brave Marines in the aborted relief effort did not stand a chance against a numerically superior NVA force that would practically overrun two platoons of A Co/1-6 Inf only a short time later. Their efforts, however, provided hope to the beleaguered CAP defenders and forced the NVA to shift their attention away from CAP Echo 4.

[This photo by Mike "Tiny" Readinger probably was taken in December 1967 at BT 016 706, looking eastward toward the village of Lo Giang. At the time of the battle on 8 Feb 68, the rice fields were about a foot tall. Soldiers from A/1-6 Inf advanced from near the trees on the left behind the sign and crossed the rice fields in the distance toward the far side (i.e., north side) of the tree line visible on the right side of the photo. Enemy mortars near a pagoda just to the right of this photo shelled them in the open as the attempted to advance across the fields. Marble Mountain is in the distance. CAP Echo 4 is located down the path/road about 800m through the village. The bodies of the valiant Marine relief force were found to the right of this photo in a drainage ditch just short of the tree line. It is believed that Marine medivac helicopters landed on the path/road to evacuate the wounded from C/1-6].

In the meantime, CPT Bradley (C/1-6) sent his 2nd platoon forward toward the village. One squad moved into the village to determine where the NVA soldiers were located. They crossed the ditch several hundred meters from where the bodies of the Marine relief force were later found and noticed a LAW pointed down the ditch as a booby trap. They blew it in place with grenades. At about 1015 hours, they spotted three NVA soldiers running away into the village. They wounded and then caught one who was trying to escape into a tunnel. He was dressed in a khaki uniform, had been hit in the shoulder and arm, and was pleading for medical help.

Just as they were attempting to question him, "all hell broke loose" as the NVA opened fire from 50 m. or less. Several NVA snipers were cleverly concealed in the tall trees that were devoid of limbs or vegetation for the first thirty feet of trunk. The squad leader was hit immediately, and then the medic (PFC Walter R. Pratt) was mortally wounded. Four more were wounded by 1100 hours. The unit was pinned down in the rice paddy area west of Lo Giang while their platoon in the village was under continuous attack.

Meanwhile, the enemy attack on CAP Echo 4 continued in earnest. The Marines in the small fortified position near the village of Lo Giang (1) reported that they were under heavy attack by large numbers of NVA soldiers. Although badly outnumbered, the CAP Echo 4 defenders were fortified with bunkers and wire entanglements.

[1968 photo of the southern portion of the perimeter at CAP Echo 4 provided by Mike "Tiny." Readinger, who was at the CAP Echo 2 headquarters as an RTO during the battle. His story on the CAP web site contains detailed information about the incredible difficulties faced by the CAP Marines.]

Because of the intense automatic weapons fire and mortar rounds that inflicted many casualties, C/1-6 was unable to advance toward Lo Giang. In the meantime, Company B, 1st Bn 6th Inf, under the command of CPT Dan A. Prather, had been flown north from LZ Gator near Chu Lai and had arrived south of Da Nang at LZ 410 at 1050 hours. At 1132 hours, they were ordered to move by truck to BT 015695 and to link up with the Marines under attack at CAP Echo 4.

Company G, 2nd Bn 3rd Marines, from LZ 410, was on the right flank of B/1-6 Inf as they moved toward CAP Echo 4. The Marines killed 7 NVAs as they advanced. At 08 1510 Feb, however, they were released to their parent unit and moved to the east of the Vinh Diem River to search for a reported 1,000-man NVA force. [The next day, Companies G and F of 2nd Bn 3rd Marines killed 107 NVA at BT 031698].

Approximately 1500 meters to the northeast, the combat action near A/1-6 was increasing. At 1132 hours, the soldiers began receiving heavy automatic weapons fire from BT 025706. A/1-6 reported receiving additional automatic weapons fire at 1136 hours. Their mortar fire into the village paid off with secondary explosions. At 1233 hours, CPT Brennan decided to "check out the village" and told his forward observer to have a fire mission "laid on the village" as they prepared to attack. In an audio tape he prepared on 10 Feb 68, CPT Brennan described the action in his own words:

"I put two of my rifle platoons on a skirmish line, followed by the CP group centered on the two platoons and a platoon held in reserve trailing the CP group by 100

meters. ...The two platoons on line covered a width of approximately 200 meters. The configuration was 2nd Platoon on the left (East) side and 3rd Platoon on the right (West) side and the 1st Platoon trailing in reserve. The weapons platoon went into action [from the cover of the NDP position in the graveyard at BT 023710]."

This photograph looking westward, shows the terrain between A/1-6 and the enemy concealed to their south. The entire area they crossed was flat and was covered by rice crops over a foot tall. To their front (i.e., southward) and along a northeast-southwest line running from BT 029708 to a pagoda at BT 021704 was a tree line. The northwestern corner of that tree line is shown at the extreme left of the above photo provided by Don Kaiser (A/1-6 Inf). [The graveyard where the mortars deployed is just to the right of this photo.] It was along this tree line that the enemy was thought to be deployed. Unknown to them was an 18" tall rice paddy dike about 100 meters north of and paralleling the trees. The enemy soldiers, who had apparently observed the skirmish line approaching the woods, low crawled out into the field and hid behind the dike. The soldiers later stated that they were "astonished" that the VC was so well concealed by the rice and small dikes.

As the soldiers of A/1-6 Inf moved southward, they came under heavy mortar fire about 110 meters from the trees. At the same time, they came under a tremendous volume of the enemy rocket, machine gun, RPG, and rifle fire from the dike only ten to twenty meters away. A furious fight began as the NVA soldiers charged across the field. The officers and men of A/1-6 later reported that the enemy leaders were easily identifiable as they were moving behind groups of seven to ten men using hand and arm signals to direct their units. In CPT Brennan's words:

"A Company was flanked on both sides by at least an NVA company on each side and was sustaining a frontal assault by another NVA company. The enemy assault element was on the line, advancing in a crouched firing position from the northwest wood line at the village. The flank enemy elements were attempting to link up at our rear, thus encircling [the unit]."

In a matter of seconds, A Co. and two companies of a unit positively identified as the 60th Main Force Viet Cong

Battalion (60% to 70% NVA soldiers), First NVA Regiment 2nd NVA Division with the 370th Hq's Company, were in a hand-to-hand battle in the rice paddies immediately north of Lo Giang (1). During the initial heavy contact, A Co. killed 78 NVA soldiers and suffered 10 KIA and 22 WIA.

The second platoon leader, 2LT Bowman, was killed in the fight but subsequently received the nation's second-highest decoration for valor--the Distinguished Service Cross. At one point, CPT Brennan received a call from the second platoon radio telephone operator (RTO), who thought 2LT Bowman was dead:

"The second platoon RTO called in a state of near panic. He said the enemy were crawling directly to his rear and each flank."

CPT Brennan observed that *"The proximity of the enemy fire was approximately ten to twenty meters at times. The enemy was attempting to intermingle with my troops having cut off our route of withdrawal."* He concluded that the *"only hope left for the company was to pull back to the mortar position and to reorganize."*

This photo of the cemetery at BT 026 710 (400 directly north of the tree line at Lo Giang) was taken by Alan Allen (A/1-6) on the day of the battle. The photo is looking westward past the clump of trees toward Cam Le Bridge and Freedom Hill in the background. The A/1-6 mortars were located near this position and fired to support the assault on the tree line to the south.

At 1415 hours, on the west side of Lo Giang, the platoon from C/1-6 inside the village popped smoke on both sides of their position. Eight sorties of tactical air support arrived from the 1st Marine Air Wing. The bombs and other mixed ordnance blunted the continuing NVA attack. The men from

C/1-6 in the western part of the village dragged their dead and wounded out, and low crawled back across the paddies toward the highway. At some point, Marine medivac helicopters were able to land on a large dike that ran perpendicular to the road and toward the village. All six soldiers were dusted off by Marine helicopters, and the accompanying gunships remained to provide additional fire support.

After the air strikes, the NVA resumed their assault from the northern side of Lo Giang, but the defenses of A/1-6 were held. Seventy-four additional NVAs were killed in the open. At 1500 hours, CPT Brennan was wounded, along with his two RTOs. Both radios were destroyed, and communications were lost with the battalion headquarters. PFC Victor Girling, an artillery reconnaissance sergeant, bandaged one of the RTOs and dragged him in a low crawl 300 m. back to the graveyard.

Not all the combat action had been confined to A/1-6. C/1-6 continued to be subjected to rifle fire and heavy automatic weapons fire. As CPT Bradley (C/1-6) assembled his platoon leaders to plan their next move, the unit came under a severe mortar barrage, and all the officers were wounded. At 1530 hours were subjected to an intense mortar attack at BT 018698. By late afternoon they had suffered 2 KIA and 28 WIA (including all officers) as they tried to move toward Lo Giang. Abandoning their rucksacks and packs, the soldiers moved out of the area and to the west of the highway, away from the precise targeting of the enemy mortars.

Company B, 1st Bn 6th Inf also ran into significant enemy resistance on the southwest side of Lo Giang. At 1450 hours, as they tried to move through the village and toward the CAP Echo 4 location, they came under small arms fire at BT 022694. At 1532 hours, they were subjected to a heavy enemy mortar barrage. In regard to the enemy mortar fire, CPT Prather's said:

"[t]he simple fact that we were operating in a wet rice paddy saved a lot of lives. Rounds buried themselves before detonation [The mortar rounds] hit right behind us within 5 to 10 feet, but they went down in the mud so far that all it did was spray our entire backs with mud and absolutely no shrapnel."

By 1615 hours, they finally located the enemy mortar position and pounded it with their own mortars. The soldiers hugged the dikes very closely and were able to crawl into good fighting positions. The enemy soldiers got up out of their fighting positions and formed online to assault the Americans. As CPT Prather related:

"That became the downfall of the main [enemy] force in doing that, in that we were hidden pretty well behind the dikes. We just cut them apart... I thought it strange looking

up and seeing these people coming and thinking, my God, they're

on line for an assault."

Eventually, the Americans counter-attacked and overran the enemy mortar position at BT 023697. They killed 30 NVAs at a loss of only two soldiers, WIA.

Fortunately, the Marines at CAP Echo 4 did not have to wait on the arrival of B/1-6 Inf. According to the official Marine historical accounts, they had managed "to hold out against overwhelming odds." At 1550 hours, they were extracted by air.

At 1615 hours, PFC Girling reestablished radio contact for A/1-6 and gave the battalion headquarters the first word of the company's situation. While he coordinated artillery and gunship strikes, the soldiers consolidated their position in the cover of the cemetery at BT 022713. Up to that point, fourteen were known to have been killed and another 35 wounded. CPT Brennan was evacuated by helicopter, and 2LT William B. Wendover assumed command of the unit.

Because of the losses and reduced strength of A/1-6, Co E, 1st Bn 6th Inf (E/1-6) was ordered to move from LZ 410 to help consolidate their defenses with A/1-6 Inf at BT 022712. Co C/1-6 also moved into their position at BT

014697. The confirmed enemy body count at that time was as follows: A - 207; B - 37; C-14; G (Marines)- 8. Ninety percent of the enemy had full web gear, including combat packs. Several had been armed with CS or WP grenades that exploded in a cloud when they were struck by buckshot or bullets. Over 100 enemy weapons were counted by A Co alone.

It should be noted that until 1430 08 Feb 68, the 1st Bn 6th Inf commander did not have a command and control (C&C) helicopter at his disposal. When it finally arrived, it was used for two hours for medivac and resupply. A/1-6 had 28 WIA and C/1-6 had 17 WIA. The C&C helicopter pilots were WO1 Edward A. Fitzsimmons and 1LT David R. Ewing of the "Minutemen," 176th Assault Helicopter Company. They flew 21 sorties into the battlefield, evacuated 31 wounded, and resupplied all companies. To quote the official After-Action Report:

"[without the courage and skill of Mr. Fitzsimmons and LT Ewing it is doubtful if all the wounded would have been evacuated prior to darkness on the night of 8 Feb 1968."

The Aftermath.

From 0820.11 to 0905 09 Feb 68, all elements of 1st Bn 6th Inf reported no nighttime enemy activity on the battlefield. Unfortunately, this was not true for the lone remaining Marine survivor of the CAP 4 relief force. He was searched and kicked several times while he played dead from his multiple wounds. He was discovered alive the next morning by Marines from CAP 2 near Hoa Vang.

[Red numbers show approximate locations where NVA equipment, supplies, and bodies were found.]

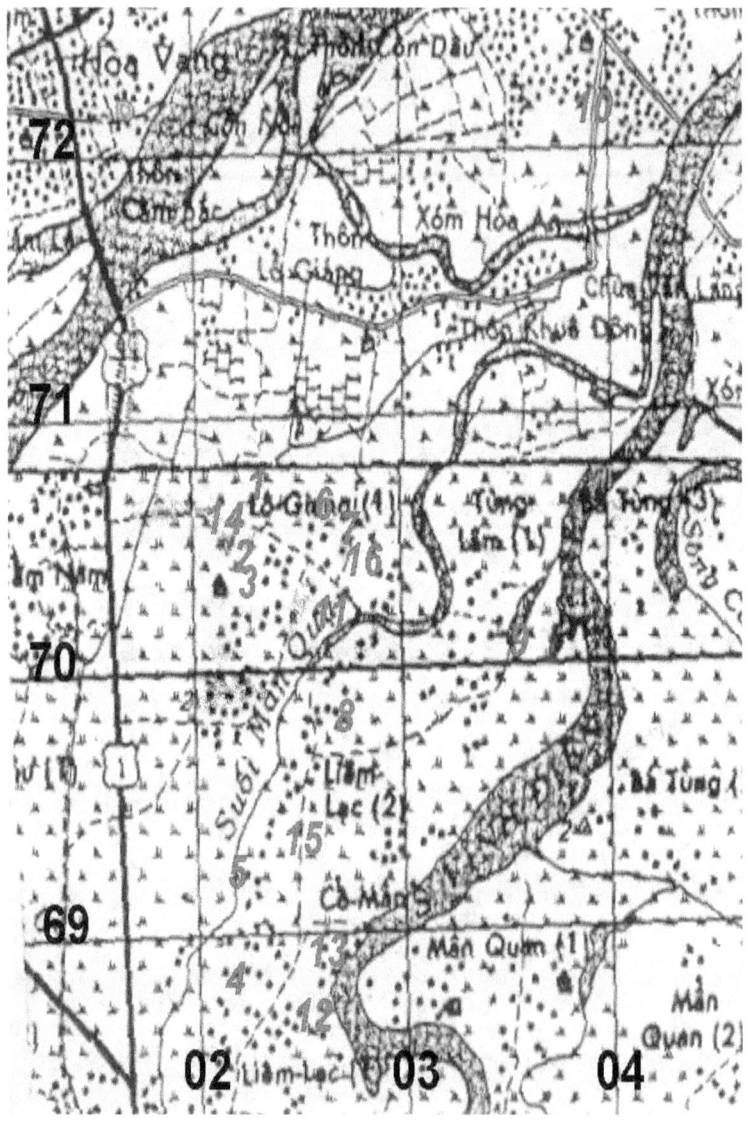

The next morning Co A and E began conducting a sweep of the Lo Giang area. While moving through the battlefield, Co E/1-6 Inf continually reported evidence of blood trails and paths through the rice where the NVA dragged away their dead and wounded.1 Near a pagoda at BT 022704 Co A/1-6 found 43 NVA bodies with web gear and packs that had not previously been counted.2 At the same

The next morning Co A and E began conducting a sweep of the Lo Giang area. While moving through the battlefield, Co E/1-6 Inf continually reported evidence of blood trails and paths through the rice where the NVA dragged away their dead and wounded.1 Near a pagoda at BT 022704 Co A/1-6 fount 43 NVA bodies with web gear and packs that had not previously been counted.2 At the same location, they found 52 Chicom grenades, 1500 rounds of ammunition, and the two damaged PRC-25 radios that had been captured from A/1-6 the previous day. Co A/1-6 had pounded the area near the pagoda with mortar and automatic weapons fire the previous afternoon.

1968 photo of the path leading through Lo Giang to CAP Echo 4 provided by Mike "Tiny" Readinger (CAP Echo 1968) [readincm@earthlink.net] The dense vegetation in and around Lo Giang and CAP Echo 4 provided ample concealment for the NVA, as shown in the photo above.

Search and destroy sweeps by 1-6 Inf troops after the battle revealed that large numbers of NVA troops had occupied practically every portion of the cover.

At 0930 hours, C/1-6 Inf found three LAWs, one M60 MG, and a box of documents at BT 022688.4. At the same time, B/1-6 found a missing soldier from C Co and the remains of another MIA.5 One or more of the dead Americans were found with their hand tied behind them, shot in the head.

At BT 025706 Company A and E/1-6 found two large piles of mixed NVA and American equipment. The piles were approximately four feet high and twelve feet in Diameter.6 Most of the equipment was NVA. At 1210 hours, C/1-6 Inf found the bodies of seven NVA soldiers with web gear and green

uniforms from the 370th Hqs Co of the 1st NVA Regiment. At 1025 E/1-6 reported from Lo Giang that they found the remains of four soldiers from A/1-6 who had been reported as MIA the previous day.7 At 1230 hours, B/1-6 found the bodies of four NVA soldiers from the 60th Bn, 1st NVA Regiment, 2nd NVA Division at BT 027699.8 At 1435 E/1-6 located 1 M-1 rifle, two M-1 carbines, one RPG MG, 50 Chicom grenades, several sets of NVA web gear, and one NVA gas mask at BT 025705. It was obvious that the enemy had been soundly defeated as it was unlike the NVA or VC to abandon bodies, weapons, and equipment on the battlefield.

The 1st Bn 6th Inf units continued to search the battlefield for signs of the enemy on 10 and 11 Feb 68.

At 1002, 08 Feb 68, Co C/1-6 found eight NVA bodies soldiers with an AK47 rifle at BT 030706.9 One of the bodies, thought to be Chinese, was determined by MI personnel and a medical team to be ethnic Noung. Cos E and A/1-6 moved into the Then Khue village area after CH47 aircraft came under fire from that area. They found two LAWs (light antitank weapons), one expended, at

BT 035716. 10 Co C/1-6 found nine additional NVA bodies in brown uniforms with web gear and AK47 magazines in the vicinity of BT 026703.11. By the evening of 10 Feb 68, it was evident that the TF Miracle area of operations was cleared of NVA and Main Force VC forces. Nevertheless, significant discoveries of weapons and ammunition continued.

At 1100, 11 Feb 68, C/1-6 found four prepared mortar positions and four 82mm mortar rounds in the hamlet of Co Man at BT 025687 that had been used to mortar A Co during the battle for Lo Giang.12 Thirty minutes later, they found a 4'x4' box of green uniforms, a briefcase full of documents, and a trench system with fire lanes and fighting positions.13 E/1-6 found two RPG MG, flares, 24 Chicom grenades, NVA pistol belts, canteens, and a gas mask near BT 022709.14 At BT 025694, C/1-6 found 29 Chicom grenades, 8 RPG rockets with boosters, 1 AK47 rifle with four magazines, and one Winchester 12 Ga. shotgun.15 At 111145 Feb 68, A/1-6 found a Hugh amount of ammunition on the eastern side of the Lo Giang hamlet.16 This included 240 60mm mortar rounds, 48 M-26 grenades, 576 12 Ga. shotgun shells, 50 claymore mines, and 3,500 rounds of .45 cal. Ammo, 847 Cal 30 round, 2,000 rounds of AK47 ammo, and 200 Chicom grenades.

Although vast quantities of enemy weapons, ammunition and equipment were discovered in the days after the battle for Lo Giang, saturation patrolling located few live enemy soldiers. Ninety enemy bodies were found at BT 044704 by Marine patrols. The absence of any signs of fighting at the location indicated that the 60th Main Force VC Battalion had retreated to the east with their dead and wounded.

On 12 Feb 16, the 1st Bn 6th Inf had completed its mission as part of Task Force Miracle in the defense of Da Nang. That effort had been costly, as the 1st Bn 6th Inf lost 22 soldiers killed and 68 wounded in action. The Marine relief force lost 12 killed, three captured as POWs [one later escaped while the other 2 died in captivity], 1 wounded, and only 1 escaped back to CAP Echo 2.

[Note: as a historical comparison, the loss of 34 KIA in only a few hours by a battalion-sized unit is a tragedy comparable to the 36 KIA suffered by the 3rd Bn 187th Inf, 101st A bn Div, in ten days of combat at the infamous battle for "Hamburger Hill" (Dong Ap Bia) during 10-20 May 1969. Other Army and Marine units also suffered greatly during the Vietnam war, but the ferocity at Lo Giang was seldom matched.]

At the end of the mission, the 1st Bn 6th Inf was extracted from the area and moved south to LZ Baldy, where they were placed under the operational control of the 3rd Brgde, 4th Infantry Division to participate

In   Operation   Wheeler/Wallowa.

They found 52 Chicom grenades, 1500 rounds of ammunition, and the two damaged PRC-25 radios that had been captured from A/1-6 the previous day. Co A/1-6 had pounded the area near the pagoda with mortar and automatic weapons fire the previous afternoon.

1968 photo of the path leading through Lo Giang to CAP Echo 4 provided by Mike "Tiny" Readinger (CAP Echo 1968)

[readincm@earthlink.net] The dense vegetation in and around Lo Giang and CAP Echo 4 provided ample concealment for the NVA as shown in the photo above.

Search and destroy sweeps by 1-6 Inf troops after the battle revealed that large numbers of NVA troops had occupied practically every portion of the cover.

At 0930 hours, C/1-6 Inf found three LAWs, one M60 MG, and a box of documents at BT 022688.4. At the same time, B/1-6 found a missing soldier from C Co and the remains of another MIA.5 One or more of the dead Americans were found with their hand tied behind them, shot in the head.

At BT 025706, Company A and E/1-6 found two large piles of mixed NVA and American equipment. The piles were approximately four feet high and twelve feet in Diameter.6 Most of the equipment was NVA. At 1210 hours, C/1-6 Inf found the bodies of seven NVA soldiers with web gear and green uniforms from the 370th Hq's Co of the 1st NVA Regiment. At 1025 E/1-6 reported from Lo Giang that they found the remains of four soldiers from A/1-6 who had been reported as MIA the previous day.7 At 1230 hours, B/1-6 found the bodies of four NVA soldiers from the 60th Bn, 1st NVA Regiment, 2nd NVA Division at BT 027699.8 At 1435 E/1-6 located 1 M-1 rifle, two M-1 carbines, one RPG MG, 50 Chicom grenades, several sets of NVA web gear, and one NVA gas mask at BT 025705. It was obvious that the enemy had been soundly defeated as it was unlike the NVA or VC to abandon bodies, weapons, and equipment on the battlefield.

The 1st Bn 6th Inf units continued to search the battlefield for signs of the enemy on 10 and 11 Feb 68. At 1002, 08 Feb 68, Co C/1-6 found eight NVA bodies soldiers with an AK47 rifle at BT 030706.9 One of the bodies, thought to be Chinese, was determined by MI personnel and a medical team to be ethnic Nong. Cos E and A/1-6 moved into the Then Khue village area after CH47 aircraft came under fire from that area. They found two LAWs (light antitank weapons), one expended, at BT 035716. 10 Co C/1-6 found nine additional NVA bodies in brown uniforms with web gear and AK47 magazines in the vicinity of BT 026703.11. By the evening of 10 Feb 68, it was evident that the TF Miracle area of operations was cleared of NVA and Main Force VC forces. Nevertheless, significant discoveries of weapons and ammunition continued.

At 1100, 11 Feb 68, C/1-6 found four prepared mortar positions and four 82mm mortar rounds in the hamlet of Co Man at BT 025687 that had been used to mortar A Co during the battle for Lo Giang.12 Thirty minutes later, they found a 4'x4' box of green uniforms, a briefcase full of documents, and a trench system with fire lanes and fighting positions.13 E/1-6 found two RPG MG, flares, 24 Chicom grenades, NVA pistol belts, canteens, and a gas mask near BT 022709.14 At BT 025694, C/1-6 found 29 Chicom grenades, 8 RPG rockets with boosters, 1 AK47 rifle with four magazines, and one Winchester 12 Ga. shotgun.15 At 111145 Feb 68, A/1-6 found a Hugh amount of ammunition on the eastern side of the Lo Giang hamlet.16 This included 240 60mm mortar rounds, 48 M-26 grenades, 576 12 Ga. shotgun shells, 50 claymore mines, and 3,500 rounds of .45 cal. Ammo, 847 Cal 30 round, 2,000 AK47 ammo, and 200 Chicom grenades.

Although vast quantities of enemy weapons, ammunition, and equipment were discovered in the days after the battle for Lo Giang, saturation patrolling located few live enemy soldiers. Ninety enemy bodies were found at BT 044704 by Marine patrols. The absence of any signs of fighting at the location indicated that the 60th Main Force VC Battalion had retreated to the east with their dead and wounded.

On 12 Feb 16, the 1st Bn 6th Inf had completed its mission as part of Task Force Miracle in defense of Da Nang. That effort had been costly, as the 1st Bn 6th Inf lost 22 soldiers killed and 68 wounded in action. The Marine relief force lost 12 killed, three captured as POWs [one later escaped while the other two died in captivity], one wounded, and only one escaped back to CAP Echo 2. [Note: as a historical comparison, the loss of 34 KIA in only a few hours by a battalion-sized unit is a tragedy comparable to the 36 KIA suffered by the 3rd Bn 187th Inf, 101st A Brigade Div, in ten days of combat at the infamous battle for "Hamburger Hill" (Dong Ap Bia) during 10-20 May 1969.

Other Army and Marine units also suffered greatly during the Vietnam war, but the ferocity at Lo Giang was seldom matched.]

At the end of the mission, the 1st Bn 6th Inf was extracted from the area and moved south to LZ Baldy, where they were placed under the operational control of the 3rd Brigade, 4th Infantry Division to participate In Operation Wheeler/Wallowa.

Additional information will be added to this account of the battle as it becomes available. To contribute additional information to this story or to make comments, corrections, etc., please contact wr9r@aol.com.

Note: A memorial service was conducted in Vietnam by the 198th Infantry Brigade on 21 Sep 68 to honor those soldiers who had been killed during the first year the unit served in Vietnam. Soldiers from the 1st Bn 6th Inf who were killed at Lo Giang were honored at that time. They include:

2LT Joseph B. Bowman
SGT Robert N. Carter
SP4 James S. Cerione
SP4 Ralph A. Dahm
PFC Amos H. Boutwell
PFC Robert L. Dykes, Jr.
PFC John I. Haselbauer
PFC Brian F. Durr

PSG John R. Poso
SGT David L. McKinney
SP4 Denton A. Carrasquillo
SP4 George R. Denslow
SP4 Lanny E. Hale
SP4 Rodney P. Troyer
SP4 John L. Jervis III
PFC Walter R. Pratt

SSG Ramon H. Gonzales
SP4 James L. Lopp
SP4 James E. Parker
SP4 John A. Wilcox
SP4 Michael Pumillo*
PFC Franklin Clovis
PFC Charles E. Hodge

SP4 Pumillo was killed later in the day, after dark. ------------------------------
----

The account of the battle was prepared by Wayne R. Johnston based on the following information: the 1st Bn 6th Inf Combat Action Report (Battle for Lo Giang) dated 23 February 1968 found at the USAIS Library, Ft. Benning, GA; oral accounts by several survivors of the battle; an audio tape made in February 1968 by CPT Francis X. Brennan while he was recuperating from wounds; a US Army Military History Institute oral history report from LTC (then CPT) Dan Prather dated 1984; Mike Readinger's story about CAP Echo 4; the USMC publication US Marines in Vietnam, the Defining Year 1968; several newspaper articles from the Americal Division newspaper, and a special report to *The Armored Sentinel* (Fort Hood, TX) provided by Tom Hall (1-6 Inf 1967 -68); and, the 198th Inf Brigade Memorial Ceremony program (provided by Alan Allen, A/1-6 1967-68). [This account of the battle: Copyright 2002].

Choose historical selections from the index at left or link to the 1st Bn 6th Inf Home Page

Echo 4